NO VACANCY

NO VACANCY

Titania Ladley

Writer's Showcase
San Jose New York Lincoln Shanghai

No Vacancy

Writer's Showcase
an imprint of iUniverse, Inc.

For information address:
iUniverse, Inc.
5220 S. 16th St., Suite 200
Lincoln, NE 68512
www.iuniverse.com

Any resemblance to actual people and events is purely coincidental. This is a work of fiction.

ISBN: 0-595-23793-2

Printed in the United States of America

For my husband, Dan, without whose love, support and encouragement this could not have come into fruition. And for my children, Tara, Zachary and Ryan. I love you all.

The greatest achievement was at first and for a time a dream. The oak sleeps in the acorn; the bird waits in the egg. Dreams are the seedlings of realities.

—James Allen
As A Man Thinketh

CHAPTER 1

From the stack of bills on her desk, she turned toward the office window and knew her world had changed exorbitantly in that one instant. The front door to Brandy's Bed and Breakfast burst open and crashed against the newly papered wall. Across the expansive foyer, with its gleaming hardwood floor, was a tall dark figure silhouetted against the raging snowstorm.

"Holy…heaven," Brandy MacKay slid her glasses down her nose and peered over the rims. "Would you look at what Old Man Winter just blew in."

"Mmm," Boomer Ludwick, Brandy's office assistant, studied the stranger intently. A giant of a man himself, he was truly impressed. "I'm already shivering in my boots."

Entranced, Brandy watched as the man sauntered toward her. As if he'd been in a mad rush, he was devoid of a coat, the wind whipping in through the door behind him, rustling his long soot-black hair. In a turtleneck and dark brown sweater, his meaty shoulders and thick chest tapered to narrow hips in faded blue jeans. As he neared, she was assaulted by brooding dark looks. An Indian, she mused.

Like a ruthless warrior on the prowl.

Her gaze fell from the snow-sprinkled hair and followed melting droplets as they began to splash into eyes of the deepest amber, like warmed whiskey, she thought as she suddenly craved a shot of liquor. Swallowing deeply, her eyes drifted down the somewhat crooked boxer's nose to the firm square jaw and full lips that were now drawn tightly in impatience.

"Do you have a room available?" he asked in a deep voice—just before his feet slipped out from under him.

She gawked in horror as the man's eyes widened a mere split second before he dropped from view. The loud thump was accompanied by a cringe from Brandy in which she blinked in shock.

"Ouch," Boomer hid behind his massive hands.

Brandy swiped off her glasses and gripped the opposite side of the office counter, sailing herself across the top until she could peep over the edge. Like a stunned hoot owl, the man stared up at the lobby chandelier as he lay sprawled on his backside in a puddle of melted snow.

Her brows drew together. Had she seen this man somewhere before?

"Are you okay?" her voice rang with concern.

The man grunted a response, then growled, "How the hell did that happen?" Sitting up, he rubbed his aching head.

"Probably my husband's doing," Brandy explained, relieved to see he was conscious. "But those bald shoes didn't help matters," she muttered to herself as her eyes studied the worn work boots.

"Your husband?" he scanned the empty foyer. The giant black man was *behind* the counter, nowhere near enough to have given him that distinct shove he'd felt across the backs of his thighs. And though she more than likely didn't know he was aware of it, he knew for a fact her husband was dead.

"Yeah," Brandy propped her elbow on the edge of the window and planted her chin in her hand, looking lazily down at him. "Ian. Some think he's been haunting the inn since I opened it almost ten months ago, right after the car accident that killed him."

The newcomer's face paled. "Haunting? That's a ridiculous—"
Behind him, the front door whooshed and slammed shut; he startled, scrambling to his feet.

"See," she slithered off the countertop. "I told you."

"That's nuts," the man decided, searching for validation from
Boomer who suddenly turned and busied himself across the office.
After an awkward silence, followed by a lengthy sigh, he asked with
undisguised impatience, "Well, do you have a room or not?"

"Double or single?" she closed the reservation book with a snap
and shoved it aside. It was apparent the man had no sense of humor.

"Double—for three," he added.

Boomer shut the computer down and began donning his coat.

Brandy raised a golden brow. "Three, huh? Well, you're in luck,"
she nudged the registration clipboard toward him, halting just short
of jamming his fingers where they were busy drumming a restless
beat on the oak surface. "We were booked, but we just got a cancellation."

"That doesn't matter," he returned, his hands now clamping at the
overhang of the window. "I already have a reservation."

Brandy pursed her lips and sent him a bland look, noting with
interest the way his chafed knuckles whitened with his restraint.
"Then why did you ask if we had a room?"

"Because it's been my experience," he leaned over the counter and
closed the space between them until his eyes were scant inches from
hers, "that hotels sometimes give away your reservations if you arrive
late."

She raised her chin indignantly, inhaling the male scent of him as
she bravely locked her stare with his molten one. "Brandy's Bed and
Breakfast is not a hotel, per se, and furthermore, would never do that
to a guest," she exclaimed.

His eyes bore into hers, hot gold melting minty green. For a long
moment, he searched her lovely face, framed like a halo by the
golden cloud of her hair, and etched every elegant curve and delicate

plane into his mind, remembering… "Would your, um, husband mind if I told you that your eyes are very sexy when you're all businesslike?"

Brandy flinched. Had his tone been laced with sarcasm? "I…well—" The radio, having been playing softly over the intercom, now blared throughout the main level of the Victorian home.

The man clamped his mouth shut as a muscle twitched over his jaw. "Don't tell me," his hand shot up to halt her words. "Your husband did that."

"Yep."

Her blinding grin illuminated the foyer. He'd seen her at Ian's funeral—had it been nearly a year ago?—but never before had he been gifted with her stunning smile. How was he going to manage to keep that expression intact and yet tell her all the devastating news?

There was a lengthy pause, the weary panther circling its target, feeling out its prey by sight alone.

"Would it be possible to have a private word with you sometime?" his eyes never left hers, and he wondered how he would look into them and tell her everything he had tucked so chaotically inside himself.

She held a breath, her brows fell. "Oh." What could a stranger possibly want to speak privately with her about? And how would she comfortably spend time alone with such a mysterious man? "Well, sure. May I ask what it's regarding?"

"You'll find out soon enough," he inhaled as his gut swirled with dread. He plucked up the pen and quickly scrawled in the registration form. Sliding it back to her, he retrieved his wallet from his back pocket and asked, "Take a credit card?"

She nodded, reaching for the offered card. When her hand brushed his, the sudden jolt that went through her, like a zap of electricity, had her gasping softly. Recovering quickly, she snatched the credit card back to a safe distance and asked in turn, "How long will you be here, sir?"

"That depends on how long it takes my…companion."

Her lips thinning, Brandy asked with controlled politeness, "How long it takes your companion to what?"

There was a fleeting stillness in the charged air. "To die," he said simply, softly.

"Excuse me?" her eyes rose from the task of swiping the plastic through the slot. Slowly, she laid it on the counter before him.

"The woman who's with me," he jerked a thumb over his shoulder as he reclaimed the card, then tucked it back into his wallet. "She's…" he breathed deeply, exhaled, "dying."

"Dying?" she gulped, ignoring the "approved" signal on the machine.

"Yes," he glanced away, but not before she caught the anguish in his eyes, the utter exhaustion. "Now may I have the key?" he asked, changing the subject abruptly.

"No—yes, mister…" she scanned his registration form, "Mr. Saxon." Where had she heard that name before? She fumbled with the key ring, finally yanking it off the hook. "Here's your key. Upstairs, first door on your right just above the office and—um, my quarters."

"Thank you," he smiled stiffly. "Now I'll go fetch my things and get everyone settled in."

With that, he spun on his heel and surveyed the lobby, glancing up to see the sweeping staircase to his right. Taking careful steps, he shivered, though not from the cold. Ghosts. Ha! Making his way safely across the entryway, he slipped out into the blustery night, his entire backside soaked.

"Boomer?" Brandy glanced about for her right-hand man. "Boomer, where did you go?"

With a shrug, she pulled down the window partition and locked up the office. How in the hell had Boomer slipped out without her noticing?

❧ ❧ ❧

In the few days since the enigmatic man had arrived, Brandy found herself oddly reflecting. Not once since Ian's passing had she taken the time—nor *had* the time—to sit down and mull over the past. But now, strangely, she began to consider what she'd accomplished, all that she'd been through.

The grand opening of her new bed and breakfast near Mystic in southern Wisconsin, with its rolling countryside and rich farmlands, had gone smoothly almost a year ago, despite the tragedy of Ian's death. It was a massive home, yet quaint and cozy, as Brandy had intended. Two-storied with peaked gingerbread gables, a catwalk tower, wraparound porch, and gleaming wide bay windows, it beckoned guests with warm hospitality. Inside, off the foyer, several arched doorways led to a tower reading room, a dining area, and a lounge complete with a wet bar. Doorways and trim had been stripped and refinished to a honey tone. Long carpet runners in golds and blues hugged the wide stairs and graced the hallway leading to the gourmet kitchen at the rear of the home. Above the entryway a balcony overlooked the lobby, paving the way for the five comfortable suites that ran the expanse of the upper level.

She'd spent the entire six months before Ian's accident renovating entirely on her own, while he'd insisted on "securing business ventures in Chicago." It'd taken some adjusting to be without him, but Brandy had adapted, accepting the fact that their marriage couldn't survive if he continued to neglect her and the inn. With a sigh, she allowed that "neglect" hadn't even been the word for it. Their marriage had been in dire trouble, and she'd been so wrapped up in the restoration of the inn, she'd ignored the signs. Bills had been forwarded to her even before his death. Credit cards she didn't know existed had listed hotel charges in Jamaica, a casino tab in New Orleans, and large purchases at a mall in Chicago, to name a few. When confronted, he'd always had an explanation. And like a fool, she'd forwarded the bills on to him at his condo in Chicago, and had conveniently tucked the nagging ache deep into her mind.

Then there was the software company he'd purchased and immediately resold months before the accident. It'd been determined that a portion of the Quantum Networking profits would go directly into Brandy's Bed and Breakfast, merely a business transaction to get the inn up and running. But she'd barely had her foot in the door getting estimates for the inn's renovations when he'd gone and sold Quantum behind her back. The small, but greatly appreciated profit checks had stopped as abruptly as they'd started.

But he'd promptly fixed all those problems by going and getting himself royally killed. The shock had long faded, and she was getting back on her feet. She accepted that an early death had been his destiny; Ian had always been a daredevil in every aspect of his unstable, volatile life.

If it hadn't been for Boomer, a widower himself, she would've had to place the inn right back on the market. An admitted former gang member, Boomer's enthusiasm matched Brandy's. He'd become an invaluable partner that she couldn't do without—and he'd been grateful for the opportunity to turn his own life around in order to provide for his young daughter, Rachelle.

Now that they had a routine down and business was beginning to flourish, she happily ignited the "No Vacancy" sign several nights a week. Feeling festive, she was able to begin preparing for the holidays ahead as November blew in with a vengeance, one snowstorm pounding impatiently on the heels of the last.

Brandy scurried to the stock closet behind the desk to retrieve a new stack of brochures. "All booked up?" she asked, kicking the closet door shut behind her.

Boomer nodded, grinning proudly. "And during a blizzard like this. You've done a fantastic job, Brandy."

Glancing up at the friend who'd been her salvation, Brandy propped one hip against the desk. "I couldn't have done it without you," she said, her eyes full of gratitude. In some ways, he'd taken over the responsibilities that Ian should have undertaken.

He nodded his acceptance. "I'm just glad to have a good job so I can finally provide a decent life for Rachelle." He began to close the registry pad and place the credit card slips in a locked box below the desk.

"Rachelle's a good kid," she smiled radiantly as she slipped out of the office into the foyer.

He called out to her through the window. "Mr. Saxon was asking to see you earlier when you were in town picking up supplies."

"Really?" she asked nonchalantly, ignoring the thud of her heart against her ribs as she loitered in the lobby, suddenly taking interest in straightening the brochures boasting local attractions, cheese factories, flea markets, camping, fishing, snowmobiling.

"Said he knew Ian." Boomer clicked a few items on the computer screen, shut it down with expertise.

Tidying the literature and adding more to each row, she nicked her finger on the wire rack, withdrawing her hand as if a snake had bitten her. "He knew Ian?"

"Mm-hm," Boomer mumbled, going about his chores, pushing the desk chair in, and placing paperwork in baskets over the file cabinet before bending to retrieve a paper clip off the floor.

When he failed to go on, Brandy's hand shot across the counter and snatched his belt loop, hauling him up against the opposite side of the front desk. "Damn it, Boom, for once could you elaborate a bit more?"

He calmly unhooked her small finger and tugged his pants down to undo the wedgie she'd given him. "That's all. Nothing more."

Her golden brows dipped suspiciously, and Boomer watched with fascination as her green eyes darkened. "That's all?"

He went back to his routine, engaging the answering machine, flipping the calendar to the following day, then turning down the lights in the back office. At careful thought to her question, he stepped out into the foyer, donned his coat, and replied, "I suspect he's just doing what everyone else is. Taking some time off, getting out of the freezing cold." To that, he added a shudder.

Recalling vividly the dark, dangerous aura that could alone melt the ice outside her inn, she asked, "Was he alone?"

"Yeah, but he did pass through earlier with a sickly-looking woman. Very protective of her," he added thoughtfully, zipping his coat.

"Hmm," she suppressed an urge to inquire further. Was the dying woman his wife? she silently wondered. "Well, I don't know the guy. And I have no idea what he'd want to talk to me about—unless it's just to offer his very belated condolences."

Boomer shrugged off the comment as he pulled down the roll-top partition to close the office window. Looking apologetically at her, he said, "Look, boss, I gotta go. I don't like Rachelle being home alone after the sun goes down."

She tossed the overabundance of brochures into a nearby garbage can. "Of course. You go ahead. Give her my love."

Snuggling down in his wool scarf and black leather bomber jacket, he then planted a kiss on her forehead. "Wrap things up yourself, Bran, and get on to bed soon. I'll see ya in the morning."

Exiting as efficiently as he managed the office, he left only one thing behind. A flurry of snowflakes that whisked in and settled in the entryway.

With a fond smile, she sighed, flung open the broom closet and drew out the mop. "Why is it," she mumbled, swirling the mop across the sleek floor, "that it's only *men* I seem to be cleaning up after?"

"Do you always talk to yourself?"

She screeched and jolted abruptly as her fist came to rest over her thumping heart. There in the dim entryway, lounging against the banister that led to the suites above, was Dante Saxon, the most gorgeous man she'd ever seen, she reluctantly concluded. As he shoved away from the baluster and ambled toward her, a vague feeling of déjà vu assaulted her. She studied the derisive features that were becoming more and more stunning with each step he took. The lean, tall, panther-like stealth of him had her breath hitching in her throat. And those shoulders beneath the green plaid lumber-jack shirt were like bricks of steel. She flushed miserably, imagining what it might feel like to run her hands over the thickness of them…

As he came nearer still, she swallowed heavily, hoping to escape the spark of those flaming amber eyes that cauterized her own with a mocking stare. Her gaze fled, came back to him, wavered, fled again.

"Well? Do you?" he asked once more, coming to stand entirely too close to her, so very close that she couldn't help but inhale the rugged male scent of him. She tipped her head back and stared against her will into the same pair of eyes that had held her briefly captive five days ago when he'd burst into her inn.

He's a married man, Brandy. Retreating a step, she planted the mop between them and clung to the handle. "Only when a man pushes me to it," she replied warily.

He studied her eyes, enchanted as they clouded to a deep sea-green. "Boomer seems to be an even-keeled man," he drawled and shrugged, wondering how a boss and assistant could casually exchange goodbye pecks.

"I don't believe I know exactly who you are," she accused, not prepared to reveal her suspicions until he anteed up. If he'd, in fact, known Ian, he'd probably known her husband better than she had.

"No," he agreed, slipping his hands into his back jeans pockets as he closed the gap, taking one more antagonizing step toward her. "You don't know me…exactly, but I'd wager you recognize me."

"I recognize you if you're laying on the floor in a puddle of mush," she shot back, shocked at her own manners, yet disappointed when he gave her a mild, unaffected look.

But he'd issued a challenge, and she couldn't resist taking the bait, if only to continue to hear the resonant deep voice as it slid like smooth silk across the small space between them, wrapping her with a sensuality she had no right feeling. Her body was definitely screaming sexual drought—it'd been an *eternity*, she unwillingly admitted.

Then it slammed into her like a meaty fist; she'd seen this man before. Even in the haze of grief at Ian's funeral, he'd been able to permeate her despair. And it wasn't until now that she allowed herself to remember it, to ignite herself in the shame of having been attracted to another man while her husband lay cold as ice in his coffin. As it were, she'd ran from the funeral parlor in an emotional panic, had fallen into a puddle of rain outside the door, and had been dragged right up into the warm embrace of a dark stranger.

Nodding, she licked her lips and said hoarsely, "Yes, you're the man at Ian's wake who pulled me from the puddle in the parking lot." Humiliatingly, she realized that she hadn't returned the favor when he'd fallen in her lobby days ago.

Watching that silky little tongue shoot out to dampen her full lips was nearly his undoing. Gripping his pockets tightly to keep from reaching out to rub his thumb over the moistness, he replied just as huskily, "And you're Ian's widow." He glanced around the lobby. "Um, the man who haunts your inn."

At that, her eyes fell from his, and she studied the handle of the mop, a lame protection against the heat that attempted to melt her heart.

"Ian's widow," she nodded slowly, her brows drawing together. "An Ian I've realized I didn't even know."

He shuffled his boots nervously. *You don't know the half of it, darling,* he thought as he explained, "As you know, I'm Dante Saxon." He offered her a hand. "I was Ian's lawyer—and his friend."

She faltered for a moment, then took the large paw and allowed him to pump her hand. Making the connection between the lawyer that Ian had referred to on occasion, and the magnetic man who had given her a smidgen of reprieve that gloomy day back in late January, her eyes went wide with understanding.

"The lawyer who advised Ian to sell Quantum Networking?" she demanded to know, snatching her hand from his before he scorched it to the very bone. "I was counting on that company as a financial assuagement for my bed and breakfast," she glared, suddenly grasping at anyone to blame Ian's idiocies on.

Dante scrubbed a hand over his face. "No, I actually advised him to keep it, even though it wasn't doing very well. But he insisted on selling, so—it being my job and all—I helped him with the legalities of finding a buyer, drawing up the documents, closing the deal."

"Without a word to me," she hissed, unable to contain her sudden bitterness. "I didn't find out until well after the fact."

Yes. He knew precisely when she'd found out. The firm he worked for, Myer and Shapiro, had been responsible for notifying her and wrapping up Ian's business. But they'd also handed some of the other responsibilities over to him, and he was currently in the process of handling the matters his own way.

Crossing to lean an elbow on the overhang of the closed front desk window, he placed one ankle deliberately over the other. "I wasn't aware that you were to be included in the dealings. *Ian* was my client. Not you."

"I see," she nodded her head vigorously. Stepping aside to fling open the broom closet, she tossed the mop in, smacking the rear wall with the handle. The thwack of the door followed.

As she sailed past him on her exit from the foyer, he clamped his hand over her arm, branding her with a heat that tempted and frightened her all at once.

"Let go of me!" she spat, eyes snapping.

Dante glanced up the stairs. "Shhh. You'll disturb your guests," he taunted, his eyes glowing like a viper about to strike. Then his gaze sharpened further, slamming into hers with the finality of an arrow being released from an Indian's taut bow. "And that ghostly husband of yours may seep out of the woodwork and begin slamming a few more doors."

"Mr. Saxon," she boiled with resentment, well aware he was mocking her. Eyes slicing down to that huge hand that continued to hold her captive, she went on, "Kindly let go of me—*now!*"

They stared at one another for an eternity, neither giving into the urge to look away, nor able to fight the magnetism that held their gazes as one.

He slowly set her arm free. "I…I'm sorry," he replied, stuffing his hands back into his pockets. His eyes narrowed then, his vision suddenly blurring as he saw an image of—Ian?—*something* swirling around her like a tornado. "I didn't mean to sound so…callous."

Dante watched, captivated, as the apparition faded and the light from the dimmed lobby chandelier played like fireflies on her glorious golden hair. The strange energy in the air was gone now, and he quickly dismissed it, studying her carefully. She was slimmer than he remembered—probably due to the combined stress of Ian's accident and simultaneously starting her own business—but still presented a luscious petite package, all wrapped up in a form-fitting navy pant suit. From his vantage point at over six feet tall, he could see down into the deep cleavage that disappeared into her white silk blouse, could smell the sweet exotic scent of her, could remember vividly the softness of her body against his that day of Ian's funeral. Yes, she was a breathtaking vision that Ian had never fully appreciated. Even the photos Dante had seen of her over the years didn't do justice to the flesh and blood of her.

"Look, I'm really exhausted," she blew out an explanation, hoping that would excuse her sudden outburst. He was, after all, a paying guest to be treated with respect—in spite of the fact that he wasn't deserving of it. "My cook's out sick, so if you want breakfast in the morning, I'll have to bid you goodnight."

He stepped further from her and bowed mockingly. "I'm never one to anger the cook. But I was simply coming for extra blankets."

And to torment me, she silently added. "At the end of the upstairs hall, there's a large linen closet," she explained as she soared around him and went to unlock a door marked "Private," positioned next to the office. "Help yourself."

Winking at her as he went to place one foot on the bottom step, he drawled, "What, you're not going to fetch them for me? None of that warm country hospitality you advertise?" With that, he sprang up the stairs whistling a tune, then was out of her view before she could think of a retort.

Brandy gritted her teeth, cringing as the house gradually quieted. She let herself into her apartment, bolting all three locks behind her. Ignoring the echoing clomp and clip of her heels on the hardwood floor, she crossed her arms over her midriff and paced furiously around the small entry hall of her living quarters.

"Arrogant ass!" she seethed, dragging a breath in.

Flinging off her suit jacket and tossing it onto the pine settee near the door, she made her way to the comfortable living room. Complete with a red brick fireplace, a plush rug under rust-toned over-stuffed sofa and lounge chair, and wicker tables at random throughout, the room was her haven after back-breaking fourteen-hour days, her comfort against…the loneliness.

Kicking off her shoes as she crossed to the fireplace, she bent and furiously tossed small logs over kindling, then struck a match and brought the flames to fruition. Kneeling before the fire, she stretched her hands to the growing inferno, reaching for the magnetic heat, yet keeping her distance for fear of being burned. The gesture instantly brought him to mind. Not her late husband, she thought guiltily as she briefly struggled to conjure up a mental picture of Ian's face, but…Dante Saxon. Eyes of fire that lured her with a smoldering heat, yet warned against pain to come, scalding pain that would inevitably be hers if she were to come too near the fire.

What was he doing here? she wondered frantically, seeing his face clearly before her in the blaze. In her fury, she'd failed to ask what it was he'd needed to speak with her about. Was he taunting her? Was he here to reveal more of Ian's deceptions? Or was he simply supporting her business as a gesture to an old, deceased friend?

No. He was up to something, she was sure of it. Well she'd find out, even if it meant kicking him out on his nice, firm ass!

With a derisive snort, she reached for a larger piece of wood, feeding the flames as she tossed it into the glowing mass. Sparks flew and flaming ashes rose into the flue.

A hand went to her aching belly as a new thought occurred to her. Could Dante Saxon have come here to inform her that Ian had sold her bed and breakfast right out from under her, just like Quantum? If it were true, then Ian—damn his black heart to hell—would've succeeded from the grave to get his way once again, to control her like a blasted robot.

She clutched her mouth, wracked with sudden nausea. Was it possible for someone to buy something and not claim it for almost ten months? It couldn't be—or could it? She knew next to nothing about real estate transactions. Had she really been that much of an idiot, sailing obliviously through their marriage for that length of time and allowed Ian to handle everything? And since the funeral, had she been so wrapped up in her anguish that she hadn't even bothered to see to details like his will and the transfer of property? She'd just assumed that as his wife, everything that'd been his was now hers. Had she been notified by his attorney? She remembered written word coming of Quantum having already been sold, but in her grief and anger, she'd pushed it aside, buried it, even forgotten about it, until Ian's lawyer had surfaced. But even now, she admitted, she needed to finally deal with the stacks of his unopened mail which remained bundled together in a file drawer in the office.

What other cruel secrets were tucked in that drawer? She suddenly felt like a fool, shuddering at the thought of it, knowing that someday soon, she would have to tackle that chore. Why hadn't she seen to the details? Why had it taken the lawyer's arrival to force her to think of such things?

And now that very crafty lawyer was indeed here—and she was quite sure he wasn't here to kick back and take a quiet vacation. Well, she was entitled to a lawyer too. The last thing she'd do is let herself be intimidated by some insolent…handsome man! She would fight him. She would never allow him to take her dreams and hand them over to someone else, just because Ian had betrayed her yet again. Never!

Tomorrow would be the beginning of her fight against Dante Saxon. True, she allowed as she went to the small kitchen, he was definitely hot. But she'd be damned if he'd waltz in here and ruin her life just because he possessed a pair of gold nugget eyes and a brick body to die for. Her heart didn't seem to beat quite right when she was too near him, and that was all the more reason to stay away—for her own health and safety.

Yes, starting tomorrow, she was going to tidy Ian's affairs up once and for all. She'd start her housecleaning by sweeping Mr. Dante Saxon right out the door—and come to the battlefield armed with a clever lawyer, just in case her temporary guest had a trump card up his bulging sleeve!

CHAPTER 2

She thought she was having a nightmare. The screeching brought her from that groggy state of blissful confusion to a painful sensory awareness. What on earth was going on up there? she wondered crankily. Buried in quilts up to her ears, the wailing still penetrated the protective barrier. It was coming from suite five directly above her.

Throwing a pillow over her head, Brandy burrowed deeper into the bed, pressing the downy softness firmly against her ear as the crying escalated.

"A baby?" she screeched, suddenly sitting upright. Dante Saxon had checked in with two other people. One a woman, and the other...a *baby?*

Oh, but of course. The baby had to be his.

Flipping the blankets away, she scooted out of bed. Slipping a white silk robe over her near-naked flesh, she rushed barefoot across the cool floor, out of her quarters, into the lobby, and up the stairs.

As she neared the door, the mewling grew increasingly louder. Brandy winced, thinking of the young newlywed couple across the hall, the elders next door having come here, in their words, for some peace and quiet, the man and wife on a getaway weekend from their own kids, and the lone woman two doors down who'd come to recover from a nasty divorce.

It was her responsibility to maintain peace and comfort for her paying guests. Armed with that thought, she rapped sharply on the oak door.

Thirty seconds, a minute. No answer. Fingers curled tightly, jaw clenched, she raised her fist to knock again.

Before contact was made a second time, the door flew open. He was standing there in sweatpants and no shirt, his bare wide chest, with its sparse dark hair over finely sculpted pectorals, had her eyes widening and the wailing baby discord gradually fading into the background. The blue sweatpants hugged narrow hips, and she purposely averted her gaze from the vague bulge at his crotch. Searching for a safe place to rest her eyes, she saw too late that his face was as dangerous as his hardened body.

His thick hair was ruffled with lack of sleep, one strand falling over his harried left brow. His eyes were like pale twinkling stars, though bags of exhaustion puffed below them. Despite the imperfection, he presented a ruggedly menacing picture as he stood there, hand on the door, attempting to adjust his eyes to the light in the corridor.

He's a married man, Brandy, she silently lectured herself, *and don't you forget it!*

Scrubbing a pair of hands over his face, he growled, "I know, I know. We need to keep it down. But goddammit, we're doing everything we can." Dante was at wit's end. Little Kyle was obviously coming down with something. He'd awakened on fire, and was virtually inconsolable.

Brandy tucked her robe tighter around her, noting with a betraying tingle to her nipples how his somnolent gaze fell to study her chest above her folded arms. "Can I get you anything…for the baby, that is. To quiet him…or her…down?" she asked, willing his attention to return to her face.

As Dante dragged his eyes from her rounded breasts pressing temptingly against the sheer white silk, the dark nipples faintly discernible through the delicate fabric, he felt his manhood unwillingly rear its deprived head. Forgetting his midnight stress, he studied intently the way her cheeks flamed with suppressed annoyance and her eyes sparkled to an enticing bottle green. Her hair was down in a shimmering mass about her shoulders, as if she'd just been tumbled by some amorous suitor. Dangerous, he silently surmised. Utterly dangerous.

"Him," he corrected with some effort. "His name's Kyle. And I'm certain he's coming down with the flu or something. He's on fire."

"Oh," Brandy nodded, stabbed sharply by guilt. "Can I get you anything for him? I have a closet in the office. There's medical supplies, medications and things. I could check and see what I have."

He sighed with relief. "That would be greatly appreciated."

"Fine. I'll be right back." She turned, halted instantly by his strong grip at her elbow.

Sucking in a breath, his eyes sliced to where her robe gaped open revealing a full curve of naked flesh, while at the same instant, he could have sworn he felt a sharp slap against the back of his head. *Ian, if that's you,* he warned silently, *you'd better find some way to get back into a* live *body—and quickly.*

"Wait. I'm coming with you," he insisted as he closed the door behind him. "I want to read the labels to make sure he gets the right one."

She gently tugged her arm from his iron-hard grasp. Clutching her robe, she studied the determination written all over his face. He truly cared about the infant, she realized. Feeling somewhat touched at the thought, Brandy nodded her agreement and headed for the stairs, knowing he followed closely behind.

His eyes fell to the swing of the gently rounded rear wrapped tightly in sheer white. Jesus, he thought with a groan as he followed her down the stairs. Holy Jesus.

❉   ❉   ❉

She went first to her quarters for the keys. Dante lounged against the wall near the office door waiting for her, unmindful of the fact that he was naked from the hips up. Brandy was reminded of a dark wolf on the prowl, his yellow-gold eyes glowing in the dark of night, waiting patiently, scoping out his prey.

With a shiver of fear laced by carnal rebirth—and a reminder that he was a married man and she a widow—she ignored the sudden hot flash that quaked her senses, and went to unlock the office door. He was near, too near, as she pushed the door open and led him to a supply closet behind the desk.

"Here," she darted in and hastily pulled an over-the-counter medicine box from a basket on a shelf filled with packs of copy paper and office supplies. "This should help."

He reached for the package and studied it in the dimness of the closet. "This is for an adult," he said blandly, tossing it back in the basket. "To stop the runs."

"Oh." Well, how was she to know what medicine a baby took? Had she ever given medicine to her little brother, Brian, all those years ago? No, she didn't think so. At thirteen, she'd have allowed her mother to take care of remedies. She'd been more interested in cuddling him.

Dante scrambled through the bin, noting aspirin, Band-Aids, Tylenol and antacids. Pushing aside a box of laxatives, he fished out a sealed box. "Ah, here we go. Infant elixir for flu symptoms."

"Elixir?" Brandy muttered.

Dante carefully considered the label, then glanced up to see a most adorable puzzled expression marring her sleepy-eyed features. His eyes locked on those lime-colored pools, and he felt his world crash around him at that very instant. *Yep, Ian,* he concluded silently, *you'd better do something fast.*

"Liquid drops. For infants and toddlers," he explained softly, raising a hand to brush a stray lock of hair from her cheek. But he didn't stop there. Tucking the tendril aside, he then shot his hand through her silky tresses and hooked his fingers at her warm nape, gripping tightly there in challenge. "Little ones can't swallow big hard things like adults can."

The quick snake-like action of his hand—as well as the double carnal meaning of his words—caught her off guard. A jolt of lightening shot through her, sizzling her from neck to bare feet. Her eyes were magnetized to his as she slapped her hands flat against his warm naked chest.

"W-what are you doing?" she gulped, pressing her palms firmly against the unyielding rigidity of those flexed muscle masses, unaware of the dim closet light flickering above them.

He wasn't quite sure himself, but muttered, "I'm reeling you in for a kiss." Pitching the medicine box back into the wire crate, ignoring the off and on flashing of the light bulb, he added, "It's what I've been wanting to do since I first laid eyes on you in that funeral parlor."

"How romantically twisted," she sneered, feeling her strength giving out against the pull of him, both physical and electrical.

He watched with a renewed thrill as her eyes narrowed, much like a hissing cat. "You're beautiful, even when you're blowing your nose from a good cry," he said teasingly, recalling her tears when she'd been oblivious to all but damned Ian and his sleek casket.

She bravely met his stare. "Get your hands off me or I'll call Sheriff Mills—and your wife."

His body jerked in surprise, then he threw his dark head back and howled, reminding her once again of that wolf, sleek and dark and…dangerous.

"What's so damn funny?" she snarled.

"I'm not married, Brandy. Whatever gave you that idea?"

She blinked. It was all she could think to do. Not married? Then who the hell was…?

When she didn't answer, only stood there in her oh-so-sheer robe that revealed more than it hid, he prompted, "I guess the baby had you fooled?"

Like hermits, the evasive woman and baby had kept to their room, so she'd been unable to confirm who was truly occupying the suite. Recalling his registration form that stated there were to be three to the suite, she said weakly, "You're here with the baby *and* the dying woman. In the same suite. What else was I to think?"

Dante moved closer, backing her into a shelf filled with stacks of copy paper. "Julie is my sister, not my wife," he clamped his eyes to hers, "and Kyle is my nephew." As an added thought, he threw out, "And the room has *two* double beds."

The false sense of security was ripped from her as his words echoed in her head, his mouth nearing her ear, nudging. She could feel the heat of him, his breath igniting her core, his bare chest plastered against her thin robe, and those steely arms as they came up to grasp the shelves behind her, caging her in.

Not married? His sister…and nephew? It was like shaking her awake, only to realize that she'd slid into another nightmare—or was it a dream? He was an extremely potent, virile, Adonis-like man—and Ian's former lawyer who'd kept all of Ian's business matters from her.

Nonetheless, he was an *unattached* man.

And she was an *unattached*…widow.

Not even a year into widowhood and she was contemplating locking his lips, those sexy full lips, with her own. What was wrong with her?

Self-disgust had her saying, "I prefer to think that things were like they appeared before."

"You mean, me being a cheating husband cornering a breathtakingly adorable green-eyed goddess in a closet?"

Those very eyes became round above blossoming rosy cheeks. "No!"

Leaning closer, he whispered a mere breath from her trembling lips, "Then how, Brandy? How do you prefer things?"

Feeling much like iron too near to a magnet, Brandy pressed her backside firmly into the shelving and struggled to breathe, "I prefer you being attached. Unavailable."

Her words revealed all he needed to know—her vulnerability, her need for defense against her own sexuality, and her obvious loyalty to a dead man who'd been an amusing friend to him, but a lousy *disloyal* husband to her.

"Oh, but honey," he whispered huskily, nipping her lower lip, "I'm very much available…and so," he sucked her upper lip between his perfect white teeth, "are you."

His hands released the vise on the shelves at her sides and slid around her to slam her flush against his hard body. The jolt—a pure flash of fire—shot through her, shocking her dormant senses into life, resuscitating her soul.

Along with it came a widow's flood of shame. It was all she could think of…except for the warm heat of Dante's hard, chiseled chest crushing her softness, springing her nipples to life, resurrecting a long-buried flame that she thought had been extinguished forever.

When the evidence of his desire sprang firmly against her lower abdomen, she became aware of a stronger sense of disgrace. What was wrong with her anyway? she asked herself before hissing, "What's wrong with you anyway?"

"What's wrong with me?" he growled like the wolf he was. "Suddenly, not a thing, darling." With that, he descended upon her, again the beast tearing ravishingly into his prey, making his long-endured hunger well known.

Brandy was unprepared for the onslaught of both the physical and the emotional assault. His lips devoured her, trapped her, gave her no route for escape. She was at his mercy—and her own. Disgrace suddenly evaporated into hunger the likes of which she'd not experienced until this very moment. Defenseless, she felt her hands slide up his warm back, kneading, exploring every taut ripple of muscle and bare flesh. She was drowning, surrendering, as he tore his snarling kiss from her lips and buried his face in her hair, finding the leap of her pulse, then trailing down the silky slope of her neck where her robe gaped open. Claiming one rigid nipple between his lips, he flicked his tongue over the silky flesh.

She felt a sob tear from deep within her throat as her head fell back against the shelving and he reached for her thigh to drag it up the side of his own. A delicious, swirling tug of fire ignited in her womb.

And it was in that position she found herself when the baby upstairs wailed in protest.

Dante's head came up with lightening speed as he released her nipple with a smack. "Oh shit. Kyle. How could I have..." And with that, he dismissed her abruptly and fished the box of elixir back out of the basket. It was then that the light ceased its strobe activity and glowed warmly.

Brandy brought herself up as if a barrel of ice-cold water had been dumped squarely over her singed skin. Humiliated, she gripped her robe closed as a rush of self-loathing brought a sting of tears to her eyes. She'd been half naked, wrapped like a harlot around a mere stranger, and a widow for not even a year. The assault was nearly fatal to her self-respect.

How *could* she?

But her answer came as swiftly as his invasion had; she took one sweeping glance of him as he turned and stalked from the closet, and there, quite blatantly, was the explanation for her temporary insanity. He was a beautiful specimen of a man, all bronzed, hard and muscled from his broad naked shoulders to the narrow waist that disappeared tauntingly into sweatpants that were loose, yet revealing. His dark hair was tousled and fell to brush the back of his shoulders, and she came to liken him to an ever transforming werewolf—one minute, the hungry yet reticent wolf stalking its prey, the next, the savage in Indian form threatening devastation on the civilized captive.

When he suddenly turned to face her as he placed a hand on the office door, a complete revelation came to her. How could she? she'd asked herself. *That*, she thought wryly as she fought to steal her own gaze from his ensnaring one, was how. No woman, widow or not, had a defense against that steely grace.

Dante's words clogged momentarily in his throat. The picture before him, a regal defiant she-god in a white robe, full bosom heaving with breathlessness, golden hair tumbling around her in disarray, clogged his breath in his chest. But it was the glistening eyes that did it, eyes that, even from the distance across the room, melted his libido like an adolescent giving into the wiles of that first glimpse at a *Playboy* centerfold. Green pools of unshed tears of shame, humiliation, and, yes, desire, reminded him of the time he'd held her in his arms at Ian's funeral. She'd wept unashamedly and given her resolve over to him. She'd incoherently thought him to be Ian come back from the dead, and he'd capitalized on that misunderstanding, pulling her protectively into his arms—and his heart.

Damn Ian anyway for the lousy husband he'd been to her, he thought, and damn himself for being captivated by photos of her. Obsession had taken a swift hold of him when he'd spied her arrestingly sexy, yet innocent photographs tossed like unimportant documents on a lower shelf in Ian's office. The infatuation hadn't let up since, but loyalty to both his best friend and his sister had kept him from chancing a meeting with the oblivious Brandy MacKay, a woman who'd had no idea that her husband had been leading a double life.

"I need to get back to Kyle," he explained with a trace of regret and irritation. "The fever, remember?"

Brandy took a shaky breath and released it. "Yes, of course," she replied frostily. "He needs something to quiet him down before he wakes all my guests."

Dante hadn't expected that bit of tartness, but he supposed she was grasping at any form of defense she could find. Foremost, though, Kyle needed him. With a nod and a quick toss and catch of the flu medicine, he said silkily, "Sweet dreams, beautiful," and slipped from the office, taking with him the heat of the night.

CHAPTER 3

Brandy ignored the feeling of apprehension in her gut. The past few days, her inn had experienced a gradual decline in occupancy. The newlyweds were on their way to The Keys, the elderly couple was now off to Canada, and the young couple seeking solace from their monstrous children had checked out this morning, commenting that if they stayed much longer, they'd be arrested for neglect. But others would come…she desperately hoped.

Tucking the metal cleaning tote upon her hip, she began the process of tidying the rooms, preparing for possible drop-ins for the night. There were no reservations—except the Saxons newest rebooking for another week—but hopefully, she would be rising in the middle of the night to check in some fatigued travelers.

The weather was putting a real spin on her business. Her cook had called in again, and her maid was down with the flu. How will I run the whole inn alone? she wondered as the fear knotted inside her. If it weren't for Boomer, bless him, she'd never swim. She'd sink like a lead balloon.

The suites, she mused as she peeped her head in each door, weren't too awfully trashed—with the exclusion of suite three. As if there'd been a wrestling match in the room, the bed was one huge mass of blankets balled so tightly that it took Brandy several minutes to disentangle the mess. With a fond blush, she knew this had been the room of the young newlyweds from New York. They'd obviously, and shamelessly, enjoyed the new delights of the marriage bed.

Several empty bottles of champagne, along with fluted wine glasses from the wet bar, were here and there, as if they'd been cast aside at that moment of passion when nothing else mattered but each other. Clearing the clutter, she wiped the small cherry dining table down, then went to gather the lone stemware that sat upon the bedside table.

"Need some help?"

Stiffening, Brandy turned to see Dante filling the doorway, one hand placed above his head on the doorjamb, while the other was hooked by a thumb in the belt loop of his jeans. He wore a long-sleeved white Adidas T-shirt that seemed to cling to every bicep, tricep, and pectoral he owned. Her lawyer hadn't yet returned her call, and suddenly, she felt defenseless against this one.

"N-no. I can handle it on my own."

Dante pushed himself from the portal, giving the door a shove as he came further into the room. His eyes locked tightly on her as she flinched at the click of the dead bolt. She was dressed in jeans and a sweatshirt, her gold hair pulled back into a high ponytail, a navy blue handkerchief tied about her head. She was a vision, he thought. Nearly as arousing as she'd been in the delicate robe several nights before.

"I'm sure you can. You're a strong woman," he said huskily, lifting her chin with a finger as he came to stand mere inches from her.

Wrenching her jaw from his warm touch, she asked with narrowed eyes, "Why are you here? What do you want from me, Mr. Saxon?"

"It's Dante, and I want nothing from you," he replied smoothly, crossing his thick forearms over his thicker chest. *Except maybe a taste of those cherry lips.*

"Spoken like a true lawyer snake-in-the-grass," she hissed, slithering from between him and the bed.

"Ouch," he winced, following her with his eyes, watching with interest the luscious rear presented to him as she bent to dust the dresser with a sudden vigor.

"That was well deserved and you know it," she accused, turning to face him and folding her own arms in mock arrogance.

"I'll give you that," he conceded, continuing to bore his intense eyes into her.

"Well?" she asked impatiently, not budging with her own stance, nor her own stare.

"Well, what?" he asked, deluding to ignorance.

"What are you doing here?" she threw out as she stalked across the room to come face-to-handsome face with him. "Why has the lawyer of my deceased, *dishonest* husband come to haunt me in my own home nearly a year following his death? He sold it didn't he?" she wailed, dreading his answer, yet craving it. "He sold this damn place right out from under me, just like Quantum, and you've come to evict me, right? You've come to inform me that there's not a damn thing I can do about it!"

He watched, intrigued as her eyes turned from olive green to flaming emerald. But more interesting were her words. "*What?*"

"You heard me!" she jabbed his chest with each word she spoke. "You heard every word I said. Now try to deny it."

He didn't know what was worse, what she was accusing him of, or the actual truth of why he'd come here. But in reality, he grudgingly admitted, she'd nearly hit the nail on the head—but not quite. He studied the pain, the raw fear in her eyes, and he knew a sudden need to protect her, to squelch the apprehension from her soul. Like a reflex, he yanked her into his arms and crushed her body against his.

"Stop!" she squirmed, her voice muffled against his chest.

He soothed, stroking her back, absorbing the sweet scent of her. "Shhh. Just take a few minutes to calm down." *And to get ready for the bomb I'm about to drop,* he thought with self-loathing.

She knew it would happen. She'd known as soon as she touched him, she'd be lost, but her temper, and that burning desire to drag the truth out of him, had had her making a dangerous mistake by zipping back across the room to stand within arm's reach. Now she was in heaven—or was it a tortured hell that she seemed to be sickly drawn to?—and could only feel the warmth of his chest against her, the sizzle of his hand as it caressed her spine, incinerating old demons, yet enticing others.

He held her there for the longest time, and Brandy concluded that it had to be paradise she was experiencing. She could hear the erratic beat of his heart, feel his muscles ripple as he caressed her from shoulders to buttocks, smell the subtle mixed scent of soap and man. The sheer bliss of being held so very tenderly, of being the center of a man's attention, had her pride fading into nothingness.

I need this! she told herself. *I need it like winter needs cold, like spring needs rain.*

Slowly, she lifted her face to stare up into smoldering eyes of restrained passion. She didn't know what this strange attraction was between her and her dead husband's lawyer, but she welcomed it somehow, and in that instant, raised up on tiptoe as her arms went around his neck. Her eyes fluttered shut as she pressed trembling lips to his astonished ones, forgetting that she'd been in the middle of an interrogation. When he groaned and surrendered all at once, so did she, and she felt the last shreds of decency flee her as she shamelessly pressed her body to his, gripping him savagely with mouth, arms, legs.

Across the room, vases, ashtrays, the coffee pot, all crashed to the hardwood floor, but neither cared, neither questioned or noticed the eerie goings-on each time they came together.

"Brandy..." Dante breathed as he crushed her against him, lowering his hands until they reached the bottom of her sweatshirt, then racing them up her back. Expertly, he released her bra, and holding her firmly against him with one hand, he slid the other around and between them to cup a full breast.

She felt the liquid fire scorch deep within her loins, and her head fell back with a feral growl. His mouth scalded her as it made a path from her jaw to that place at her neck where her pulse leaped frantically with every touch, every thought of him. In one swift movement, he had her sweatshirt on the floor and the handkerchief ripped from her head. With his teeth, he dragged her bra straps down, revealing bare shoulders set fittingly above the perfection of her ripe breasts.

He was mesmerized by the treasure he was uncovering. She was more beautiful than he'd ever imagined, a paragon of art, a masterpiece. *Ian, what a fool you were,* he thought, as he swept her up in his arms and crossed the room to lower her to the bed she'd just made.

Taking in the beauty of her bosom, thrust high even as she lay on her back, he examined the perfect pink-tipped nipples, watching in carnal wonder as they hardened before his very gaze. Throwing one leg between hers, Dante pinned her with a smoldering look before raising the twin globes and burying his face between them. Torn between the identical beauty of them, he went from one to the other, raising, kneading, suckling, swirling his tongue around each nipple until Brandy's moans became so vocal, he was forced to abandon them for the lusciously full lips that were pursed in ecstasy.

His mouth came over hers in a gentle, yet controlling swoop, and Brandy felt a tug from her very toes as his tongue darted in, out, around hers. Her nipples, still damp from his previous feast, were taut against the soft cotton of his shirt. Her arms came around his neck, drawing him closer, deepening the kiss until she moaned with the feel of this renegade of a man invading her senses, claiming her, sucking the very life from her with a mere kiss.

On the prowl, Dante broke free and rose beside her on the bed, looking down at her trembling body with a hot, intent gaze.

Expertly, he unzipped her jeans, baring her slim abdomen before him like a shrine.

"I want you, Brandy," he murmured quietly, feeling himself go painfully hard. "I've wanted you for so long, so damn bad I can think of little else."

Her lips curved ever so slightly and she reached up to hook her hand behind his neck. With one hard tug, she yanked him down until his mouth slammed against hers. His hands were everywhere, on her, around her, slipping into her jeans, caressing and massaging in one devastating sweep. She cried out when he slid one finger into her wetness, then ducked his head to claim one hardened nipple between his teeth.

She was gasping, rocking, bucking against his fingers as he deftly pumped her. Her hands released his head where her fingers had become entangled in his hair, to slap the bed at her sides. Her fingers curled into the quilt, and she barely noticed the ripping noise as the fine threads snapped against her fevered strength. Frantically, she searched for the hem of his shirt and began to pull it over his head.

In so doing, his hand left her briefly, leaving her empty and discontent, a craving ache burning in her crotch.

Hungry, he returned to her and his mouth began to follow the path his hands had previously taken. He had to see all of her, get in her, taste her. Long deprived of a woman, having been busy as nursemaid to his sister and nephew, he felt much like a teenager in the back seat of a car. It wouldn't take long, he thought, as he ran his tongue along the crease under one breast. But he wanted to please her, to focus on her needs, to set his own aside so that she'd know only him, forget all else that'd come before him.

Forget damned Ian.

Brandy's thoughts were much the same, sure she would go mad if she didn't have him. Ten months of celibacy had wreaked further havoc on her senses than she'd realized. A mere flick of his tongue over her flesh had the potential to bring her to climax. He was demanding, yet gentle, well-schooled in the art of love, yet clearly fighting for control, a quality that, in and of itself, was a fatal aphrodisiac.

She couldn't breathe, couldn't think, couldn't speak, so consumed was she with the white-hot power of his magic hands, with the feel of his corded muscles under her hands. With great effort, she finally panted, "Dante…"

"Yes, babe," he replied huskily, impatiently, as he made his way further down the flatness of her belly to flick his tongue into her naval.

"Now," she breathed heavily, her core aching painfully for him. "Take me now."

Without notice, the television flicked on and began to blare. But nothing, not even the spirit that watched angrily, could dissuade them from their course.

The pleading, innocent tone caught Dante off guard. His eyes rose to meet hers and he saw complete trust and need in them. Like a wolf tempted by succulent meat, he was unable to take another path away from his prize. Coming over her, he settled between her thighs, crushing the hardness that'd sprang inside his jeans, against her apex.

"I've got to have you, Brandy," he vowed as his hands lowered to grip her waistband ready to divulge of the barrier. He prayed she wouldn't resist, silently begged her to give him the response he desperately needed. "It's time to let him go."

Her eyes flew wide. The meaning of his words diffused into her like a bitter medication. *What was she doing?* Rising on her elbows, she scooted from him, frantically looking for an escape. "No!" she choked on the word, already having been scorched with the feather-soft stroke of his tongue against a betraying nipple.

"Look at me," he ordered with painful restraint as he held her in place.

Clamping her eyes tight, she continued to struggle weakly, but he remained between her thighs with little effort. "Brandy," he said, then again, "Brandy!"

When she stilled her movements and her eyes slowly opened, Dante's heart tumbled out of his chest. Like glimmering gems in mountain spring water, she held his gaze with hers. He saw the want, the pain, the loneliness aching to be released—the fear and indecision. And he saw something else, something he didn't care to define at the moment.

"It's the first time…since Ian passed away?" he asked, astonished, yet sure of the answer.

She looked away, abashed, and slowly nodded her head.

"Look at me," he ordered gently.

She obeyed, gazing at him with a mixture of passion and shame.

His eyes never leaving hers, his hand dove back into her pants to locate the honeyed wetness. She gasped, a cry of desire escaping her—and indecision was forgotten in the pulsating ache that assailed her.

She was on fire. She didn't care to explore the fact that she'd never experienced this intensity before, not when the sweet mixture of utter embarrassment followed immediately by wicked, wicked desire beset her. It crashed into her, invoking a throbbing sensation the likes of which she'd never felt before. And consequently, it left a relentless craving, a sense of wanting—no, *needing*—much, much more.

"I want to see your beautiful eyes when you reach your peak," he said softly, sinking a finger to the hilt inside her.

She came off the bed in a flurry of moans and gasps.

Warmed by the golden blaze of his gaze, she was dying for the throbbing deep within her to be fed and sated. He was the picture of roguish bad boy, ready to strike, ready to seize. Her hands reached up and tangled into his thick dark hair. It was a deliciously lurid feeling to be overpowered by him, to abandon all scruples in order to experience the lust he was introducing her to.

Though she heard a distant angry voice—was it Ian's?—she ignored it. She needed this, needed Dante. She desperately needed him to claim her, to cleanse her of her damned widowhood, to liberate her and bring her back to life.

"There," she replied huskily, her eyes seductively boring into his. Enflamed, it seemed a wanton took her over, possessed her until she continued, "You can see my eyes now. So what are you waiting for?"

He groaned in response and managed to get her pants down until he could barely see the neatly-trimmed patch of golden hair. Expertly, he moved his finger within her and simultaneously ran his thumb rhythmically over the hardened bud. Brandy cried out and sighed, her eyelids fluttering, battling to remain locked on his. Her hips rose with her passion.

Holy hell, Dante thought with a mental gasp. She was tight and sleek, and he was certain he'd never felt a woman quite so sweet before. Warning lights ignited in his head, and he ignored the sudden sensation of hands pulling him from her—Ian's hands? he wondered briefly. But nothing short of the devil himself, Dante knew, could deter him from his purpose.

Brandy's knees came up and she clamped them tightly together. She was soaring without effort, could see, feel, taste, even hear the onslaught of release as it reached for her. Every muscle in her body tensed, ceased to move. Her breath caught, and she felt her hips rise yet again to meet his expert hand.

He heard her soft moan as her knees fell apart and she suddenly convulsed against him, reaching her release with the urgency and abandon of a woman long denied. Though he was painfully hard, he refrained from ripping the remainder of their clothes away and plunging himself deep within her, for he saw the shame return as soon as the waves of passion ebbed.

Brandy crashed back to reality. Had she just allowed the lawyer who'd duped her, to dupe her again? Had she truly just done that? In one of her suites set aside for guests? *You stupid, stupid fool!* her mind echoed, scolded.

Slowly he stretched out beside her, tucking her shivering body against his rigid one. He stroked her from shoulder to thigh, soothed, calming the self-mortification that she now exuded. Lying there flushed and stunned, she refused to look at him, refused to accept what she'd just allowed him to do to her.

After several long, quiet moments, he gently tucked the bedspread about her where she lay deathly still, save for the faint panting. "That's only the beginning, doll," he drawled, looking down at her dazed expression. "And there's nothing to be ashamed of." Wavering momentarily, he gently released her, sat up, plucked up his shirt, then rose and strolled from the room, leaving her to absorb what had just passed between them.

The tears came swiftly. Humiliated, Brandy shoved aside the vivid sensation of his tongue on her, his fingers in her, his aura draped all about her like a sensual cloak of power. Even now, minutes after his departure, she was burning for his touch, desperate for one more caress. And it was with that thought that she cursed the day that Ian MacKay had ever purchased this godforsaken inn for her. She longed to be back in New York where they'd lived before buying the bed and breakfast, where life had been so routine and bustling. She longed suddenly to be far, far away from Dante Saxon.

CHAPTER 4

Thanksgiving week brought with it two back-to-back blizzards dumping nearly a foot of snow and drifts across the deep south of Wisconsin. The inn was isolated on a country lane ranking low on the county's list for clearing.

Several reservations were canceled. Boomer and the part-time cook and maid were forced to call in, unable to make the treacherous journey to work. Brandy became a jack-of-all-trades, adept at cooking and cleaning. But the Saxons called out for nothing, tending to their own needs, Dante pilfering in the kitchen late at night for their meals.

Snowbound, she'd been unable to make the appointment with her lawyer, and her stomach twisted painfully at the thought of being defenseless—defenseless in *every* way—against the ruthless, devastatingly sly Dante Saxon. And she avoided him as if he were an epidemic spreading around her, invading the immunity she thought she'd had against any other man but Ian.

Thanksgiving morning dawned frigid with pink-tinged gray clouds on the horizon, threatening yet another snowstorm. Oaks and maples strained to uphold the weight of fresh snow, their dark bare limbs near to snapping in the frosty air. Firs and pines held steadfast green as blue jays and cardinals fluttered across the white-tipped limbs, sending a dusting of chalky powder about.

The inn wore a bright crisp cap over rooftop, dormers, and castle peaks. Walkways and the drive remained smooth as a skating rink, untouched by shovel or plow. A thick wisp of smoke puffed from the stone chimney, fading into the gray of the sky. Windows trimmed with lace curtains revealed a warm orange glow from random rooms on the main level. The upstairs windows gave no evidence of life, save one lone light radiating from suite number five.

Brandy bent to shove the turkey back into the massive commercial oven, closing it reluctantly as she savored the rush of heat. The scent of cinnamon and cloves wafted the air as the pumpkin pies baked. Yeast rolls were rising over the stove, while a heap of potatoes filled the chrome sink for a rinse and peel. Cranberry salad, whipped topping, pecan pies, and cherry-topped cheesecake all remained chilled in the refrigerator. The wine cooler was stocked, as usual, with some of the finest red and white Wisconsin wines.

The dining room was parted from the large kitchen only by a lengthy breakfast bar. Brandy scanned the room and double-checked the table. A white linen tablecloth was covering the long claw-foot maple antique. Upon the table was a harvest cornucopia centerpiece flanked by bronze candlesticks; rich burnt orange candles topped the heirlooms. She set out her finest china and silverware, then placed fluted crystal wine glasses above each floral plate. Removing one chair, she went to a corner and returned with a wooden highchair, then scooted it up before one of the settings. She had yet to see the baby, though she'd lost many night's sleep with his fussy awakenings directly above her quarters.

A baby. If only she'd been able to conceive...

Stepping back from the baby seat, she shoved the "if onlys" deep into her heart where they would remain buried.

She had a job to do. She had guests to tend to.

The Saxons would be her only dinner guests. Butterflies danced in her stomach as she smoothed the apron over her slacks. She'd have to face *him* again, look into those eyes the color of cool white wine, yet flaming with a soul that could be read like a carnal book. She had to keep things under control. She'd managed to avoid him the past week or so. And yet with a mere thought of him, her body would betray her with a relentless aching flame deep inside, begging of its own accord for his kiss, his touch.

She'd dreaded this day, forced by business etiquette to be alone with him, alone but for his nephew and sister whom she'd yet to meet. But never again would she allow herself to be so isolated in a room that he'd have the chance to devastate her so thoroughly. She'd damn well locked each suite behind her from that day on, loathe to be caught unawares again as she attempted to clean and keep her business afloat.

It had been a mistake, she was well aware. Nearly a year of abstinence had driven her to abandon all scruples and pride to a man who was as hazardous as walking a tightrope above a pit of cobras. If she fell, if she made one wrong move, she'd be destined to a painful, poisonous life of loneliness. She dreaded facing him, was sweating now with apprehension over being in the same room with him for Thanksgiving dinner.

Soon she would see him up close and personal. No more dodging one another, no more strategically planning to avoid him by transferring the phones to her quarters early in the afternoon. No more ducking into the nearest closet at the sight of him entering the lounge. Sooner or later, the time would come when she'd have to face him again, and that time was finally upon her. As paying guests, the Saxons deserved a Thanksgiving spread.

What would she say? What would *he* say?

The questions had plagued her since that day she'd become an innkeeper-turned-harlot. Just thinking of his magic hands, as she'd done countless times over the last ten days, had her cheeks smoldering and her heart racing. He'd been an attentive lover, intense, unselfish. Never before had she experienced such a profound touch, mystical yet laced with an irresistible dark side she couldn't quite put her finger on. And selflessly, he'd left without pleasing himself, and had had the decency since then to show her respect by staying clear.

It was for the best; it had to stop before it started. There would be no more. It was ridiculous, utterly shameful to become the lover of her dead husband's friend and lawyer—deceitful lawyer at that—right here in her own home, under the same roof where she strove to be a wholesome hostess to her guests.

Some hostess you've become, Brandy MacKay! she thought with a snort of self-disgust as she returned to the kitchen and began peeling the potatoes.

"Need an assistant?"

Her head came up, though she didn't turn. "No," she paused briefly. "Thank you."

Dante scanned the kitchen. Several food preparations were in progress. "You're a liar."

Gripping the vegetable peeler tightly, Brandy whirled to face him. "I beg your pardon."

Just as her words were ground out, she was assaulted by the picture of him leaning against the breakfast bar, one ankle over the other, and the most adorable blue-eyed baby she'd ever seen clinging to him. The child's hair was as blue-black as Dante's, his skin the same bronzed tone, but the eyes, the eyes were as different as fire and ice. Dressed in a miniature blue sweat suit, he was an angelic bundle of pure innocence. How could such a sweet little tot have caused her such cranky thoughts in the middle of the night?

Dante surveyed her from head to toe. She was wearing khaki slacks and a snug harvest-colored sweater beneath a chef's apron. Her hair, pale under the florescent lighting, was swept up in a haphazard mass at her crown with wisps escaping about her nape. Eyes as green as grass sparkled with first apprehension, then an instant maternal instinct as she devoured his nephew. Suddenly, he found himself wishing she'd consume him with the same intensity, the same unbridled emotion, and he wondered why he hadn't brought Kyle out sooner.

"It looks to me as if you could use some help," Dante tried again, shifting the baby to his other side.

Brandy dropped the potato and peeler in the sink and glided forward, her eyes glued to the child as he warily eyed her approach. "Aw, what was his name again?" she asked breathlessly.

"Kyle." Dante inhaled the sweet scent of her over the aroma of cinnamon, nutmeg and roast turkey, could feel the energy around her as she came to stand directly before him.

She smiled softly. "Kyle." Raising a trembling hand, she ran the back of her fingers over the chubby cheek. The toddler buried his face in Dante's neck, and the familiar whining of the last few nights returned.

Dante rubbed a large hand over the tiny back, instantly soothing the cries to faint whimpers. "He's very shy…at first."

"He's very…" she swallowed heavily, reaching to run a light hand through the soft straight hair at the back of Kyle's head, "adorable."

Kyle squirmed at the foreign touch and climbed further up his uncle's massive chest. Dante patted his diapered rear reassuringly, allowing Brandy to continue the petting. "Julie needed a break," he explained. "She's decided to join us for dinner. She's doing the female primping thing."

Would she recognize Kyle? Dante wondered, watching with mixed emotions as she consumed the child with a hungry stare. *Would she see the resemblance?*

Brandy tore her eyes from the small bundle, only to have her gaze stolen by yet another perfect picture. Dante's eyes were blazing into hers, searing her with something…something heavily charged with emotion—or was it guilt?

"That's wonderful," she nearly whispered, her eyes imprisoned by his. "I'll finally get to meet her."

Kyle let out a sudden scream and threw his arms around Dante's neck. "Ma-ma, Ma-ma, Ma-ma," he babbled, rocking his body against the wall of Dante's chest.

"He wants to go back to Julie. I was hoping to give her a break."

With some effort, Brandy freed her eyes from his and went to prepare a plate of cinnamon rolls and fruit for him to take upstairs. "What a thoughtful brother you are." *And what a strange set-up you two have*, she thought as she tackled the task of providing her guests with a continental breakfast in their suite.

"If you need some help—"

"No," she cut him off, setting the covered plate and jug of juice within his reach, then returning to the sink to shave the already pared potato. *Keep your distance, Brandy*, her mind screamed. "I've got things under control. Dinner will be ready at noon sharp. I'll see you and your sister…and Kyle, then."

"You're sure?"

"I'm sure," she replied with more ice than intended.

Her rigid back told him more than her words: Stay away until social graces dictates otherwise—or maybe, forever. Plagued with vivid memories of her fiery response to his touch, her sweet scent, her cries of abandon, he'd accepted that it was inevitable. They were wrong for each other—Julie's shocking news would see to that. With a sigh and a tight knot in his gut, he accepted her refusal and slipped from the room, making his way upstairs. As truth would have it, Julie needed him far more anyway.

"Julie," Dante approached his sister from behind, placing his hands on her bony shoulders and locking eyes with her in the mirror. "You don't have to do this. You need your rest."

Licking cracked lips, she beheld her brother's image with sunken brown eyes, her once exotic features now ashen and gaunt. "I have to do it for Kyle."

Gently massaging her fragile neck, Dante growled, "How many times do I have to tell you, I'll deal with it. I'll explain everything to her." *Everything within reason.*

Inwardly, he was panicking. Julie had just sprung a new angle of her plans on him. She'd originally planned to come here anonymously to spend her last days where she hoped her son would live his life. He'd agreed to let her live out her short life the way she desired, and had intended on steering clear of the whole situation, of Brandy—until he'd walked right into her front office and gotten lost in those leafy pools of raw emotion. True, he'd been infatuated by her photos, but never could he have guessed that his life would shift so dramatically when an image on paper faded into reality. Everything had changed, swirled into a chaotic knot in his belly, in a matter of minutes.

And now, as if that weren't enough mind-altering facts, Julie was going to tell Brandy everything, she was going to make shocking demands of her, and she was going to let the hissing cat out of the bag and shred Brandy's newly-patched world to pieces again. And Dante, like the fool he'd been, had brought her here thinking she'd merely wanted to be nearer to Ian. He didn't know what he'd been thinking, agreeing to such a bizarre scheme, allowing Julie's tears to get the better of him.

"She was Ian's wife. I owe her a personal explanation."

"You don't owe anyone a thing. And you never told me you were going to spring this on her when I agreed to bring you here. So, please, let *me* handle it."

Running a brush through her sparse black hair, all that was left of the effects of radiation and chemotherapy, Julie shoved a floppy-brimmed hat on until her eyes and ears were barely detectable. Raising a stubborn bony chin, she replied with finality, "No, Dante, *I* will handle it. And as far as coming here goes, would you have brought me if I'd told you the truth?"

Studying her reflection, he saw only the vibrant healthy woman she'd been before the cancer had infested her body. With a sigh, he went to examine his tiny nephew in the portable crib. He was lying on his stomach with his legs drawn up, cheek pressed against a pillow. In sleep, he suckled on a thumb, his dark brows drawn down, as if his young mind worried over his own uncertain future. An awesome responsibility ahead, Dante thought with a clenching in his abdomen, but he would do anything for his sister and her young child.

Lowering himself to the bed, Dante rested elbows on knees, clasping his hands together. "She's fragile, Julie, almost as fragile as you. She knows *nothing* about you and Ian. And especially Kyle..." he glanced down again at the oblivious sleeping cub. The secret behind his heritage was surely going to stir up some shit. Why in hell had he agreed to such a demented plan in the first place?

Julie swiveled on the cushioned dressing table settee. Her hollow eyes somehow mustered up a hopeful twinkle. "Are you starting to have feelings for her?"

Dante shot to his feet. "Oh, no you don't, Jules. Don't you even go there."

"Well?" she sneered, coming shakily to her own feet. "Do you want me to wait until I'm in my grave before I secure my son's future? Do you want me to float around like a fuckin' ghost and haunt you until I know Kyle is taken care of?"

Her words, always so brash in that Julie sort of way, weren't what caused him to snap. It was the *direction* of her words. "Stop it, just stop it!" Dante snarled, clasping his head and pacing. "You know I'll take care of him. I would never abandon him. He has a future with me. *I* want custody of him, Julie! Don't you dare turn him over to a woman he doesn't even know," he snarled, baring his teeth.

She made her way unsteadily across the room until she stood before her stubborn brother. Placing a cold, thin hand against his cheek, she said in a raspy voice, "But I want him to have a mother,

Dante." *And a father too, if things go as planned,* she thought slyly. "Can't you see that? Ian's wife would be the perfect mother. She loved Ian. She will love his son."

The muscle in his jaw twitched, and she dropped her hand as Dante sighed. "He's not *her* son...and he has a mother already."

Below the brim of her hat, dark eyes simmered with sudden unshed tears. "But I won't be here, goddammit!" she clenched her fists. "He will be motherless if you have anything to do with it. And that breaks my dying heart!"

Dante turned his back on her, went to the window and studied the ruffled curtains drawn against the dreary cold of the late morning. Peering through a crack, he could see the covered sidewalk and driveway. He should go shovel it. He should just get the hell out of this godforsaken isolated inn!

"We did just fine without a mother," he said pointedly, suddenly flinging the curtains aside. Claustrophobic. That's what he was becoming, being cramped in this room for weeks with Julie and Kyle and all that talk of death and securing futures. He had to get out, get some air before *he* died.

"No, we didn't—I didn't—and you know it."

"Look, I can't talk about this anymore," he turned to find that rigid stance of hers back and the tears gone. Tough Julie till the very end.

She crossed her frail arms over her flat chest, a chest that only months ago, had been as ample as Dolly Parton's. "Fine then. Run like you always do."

Dante's teeth ground together. It was the only response he had before he did just that...he ran until the demons of hell were chased away by the frigid Wisconsin cold.

Brandy sat in the bay window seat in the guest living room, her chin resting on drawn up knees as she waited for the stove timer to draw her back to the kitchen. It was dim in the room as pale clouds outside churned to an ominous gray. Through the crack in the wispy curtains, she furtively watched as Dante attacked the driveway, flinging snow to first one side, then the other. She could hear the scraping of metal against concrete as he victoriously cut through inches—possibly feet—of snow and ice. He was a man on a mission, a man boiling with hidden emotion.

He was, most definitely...a man, she thought guiltily as her eyes rose from the work boots to the Levis that hugged his body so perfectly, to the heavy jacket that he now ripped off as a sweat formed over his scowling brow. Beneath the jacket he wore a plain blue T-shirt that clung to his perspiring torso, revealing every taut muscle, every rippling bulge as he labored over her driveway.

She could well remember the feel of every plane, every hardened hunk of flesh under her trembling hands...

Furiously, white puffs of breath shooting out like a raging bull, Dante leaned on the shovel as he ripped one glove from his hand with his teeth, then the other. Tossing them upon the pile he'd just formed, he bent to continue his ministrations, working his way across the concrete pad until he reached the sidewalk that split off to round the side of the inn. It was an enormous amount of area to cover, but at the rate he was going, he'd have it all done in no time.

Like an obsessed teen, her gaze devoured him, and she was grateful for the snow to have drawn him out where she could privately watch him without his knowledge. She should go to him, she knew, and insist that he leave the work to her hired staff—when they were finally able to make it to work—but she hesitated, seeing the determination on his ruggedly handsome face, instinct telling her it was wise to allow him to blow off his steam, to just watch him and wait...

Shaking that thought aside, Brandy focused on the scratching of the shovel, could see him vividly as he bent and tossed snow, muscles rippling, mind boiling. But now she allowed herself to see an entirely different man, a man tormented by the pain and suffering of a loved one. A man agonizing over the impending loss of a sister and the toddler who would become motherless.

Yes, there would inevitably be a couple of vanquished hearts. But where was the child's father? Sympathy filled her heart as she thought of precious little Kyle with his azure eyes and midnight hair being shunned by his father, then being torn from his mother's arms by merciless death. She could identify with that child even now, before the heartache began for him. She'd lost her father—but that'd been her own fault, as Maxine, her mother, took resentful delight in reminding her. And then there was Brian…a little brother lost almost sixteen years ago, snatched from below her very nose, gone forever, and all because of her own carelessness. Still, the one question plagued her: Was he still alive?

The buzzing of the oven timer brought Brandy back to the here and now. She had a Thanksgiving dinner to serve to her guests. With a heavy weight in her heart, she made her way into the kitchen to disengage the timer. Reaching for the fluffy pot holder mitts, she slipped them on and bent to pull the roasting pan from the large commercial oven.

The aroma of honey roasted turkey and stuffing filled her nostrils. Thanksgiving had always been a treasured holiday for her. Even after Brian had been kidnapped all those years ago, Maxine had put aside her antagonism—just for a day, one treasured day—and allowed their family to have a tolerable day of feasting.

Christmas was an entirely different matter.

"Mmm, smells wonderful."

The voice, seductively deep, was so close, the roasting pan nearly slipped from her hands as she screeched and turned on her heels. "Don't *do* that!"

"The food smells great too," he jested, leaning over the fat basted turkey and inhaling deeply.

His eyes were sparkling like nuggets of gold betraying a mood that was altogether different from the man who'd furiously been shoveling her walk. His hair was slicked back, as if he'd ran a hand through the perspiring thickness of it, and he wore only the Levis and the sweat-soaked shirt. Every bump and bulge of his torso, and oh God, those pecs, were emphasized by the damp fabric. It was indecently unsettling, and Brandy abruptly turned and slammed the turkey onto the stovetop.

"Dinner will be ready in fifteen minutes," she said tersely, keeping her back to him. "Could you inform your sister?"

Dante studied the rigidity of her back, the slim petite length of it, the way it subtly lowered itself through the close-fitting sweater and into those snug slacks. His hands flexed now in torturous remembrance of that firm rear in his hands, pressing her against him. His eyes rose to the graceful column of her neck where she had swept her hair up in an elegant clip, and he found himself drawn there, recalling clearly the sweet taste of the tender flesh. Helplessly, aware he was playing with a dangerous inferno, his arms came around her from behind and he placed a soft kiss under one ear. He felt her briefly stiffen.

Pulling her closer, flush against his already hardening crotch, he whispered, "I can't help myself. You're so sexy, so beautiful. I've missed you."

Brandy's eyes fluttered shut as the rush of warm desire flooded her senses, centering deep into her abdomen. "Please Dante. This isn't right. Not again…"

"How can it not be right?" he queried huskily, moving to devour the other side of her neck. "You deserve to be happy again. And I know I was able to make you happy when I…touched you."

She was crazy for allowing it. But her body was aching for his embrace…just a touch. Relaxing against him, she accepted that he was a magnet, and she the softest, weakest form of steel alive.

A distant slamming door and a whirl of cold air went unnoticed by them both as Brandy's toes curled beneath her, and one traitorous arm came up to hook at the back of his damp neck. When he felt the subtle resignation, he pulled her closer, his mouth tracing the side her jaw, searching.

"I've got to make the gravy," she breathed heavily, battling fires that blazed deep in her core. "This is insane," she whispered as she released her hold at his neck, allowing him to spin her around, crushing her frontally against him. His mouth came down hard on hers, and she gave as she took, liberally demanding her own ascendancy, accepting him just for one more taste.

Dante felt her full surrender, and with it came a release of energy that singed him to the very depths of his heart. Her arms slid up to his neck once again, and he absorbed the strength of her emotions as she moaned deep into his mouth, running her fingers madly through his wet hair. This woman, this witch who'd had him charmed from afar for years, spellbound by a mere photograph, was his weakness. He'd become ever more captivated by her, and increasingly perplexed as to how a man could deceive such a warm, vivacious, and beautiful woman. And innocently, she'd been oblivious to her husband's infidelity with Julie.

But wasn't he deceiving her as well? Was he just as guilty as Ian had been?

The part he himself had played in the deception—and was playing now to an extent—well…he just refused to think of it now, not now when he had her willingly warm and pliant once again in his arms.

Brandy was lost in the golden aura of him. Like the hunting Indian stalking his prey, he snared her in a trap of passion, dangling the bait of his enigmatic expertise before her, around her, in her. She was the bewildered doe in the forest leaping into the seduction of his ambush, soaring over limb and meadow, reaching naively for fulfillment in a pitfall of desire.

His lips slanted over hers, fitting like a puzzle, exploring every curve and interlocking crevice of her mouth. She reached for him with tongue, arms, fingers, and shamelessly, with her legs as she felt one limb helplessly slide up and around his thigh. With a guttural an, his hands glided in unison down her back to cup her bottom, supporting her in her weakness, bringing her higher, closer to the heat of him. She accepted the flurry of things as one of his strong hands rose to grasp the mass at the back of her head, pulling the clip from her hair and tossing it carelessly across the floor.

Silken gold tresses fell over his hand as he gripped her hair and pulled her head back, ripping his lips from hers and burying his face in the arch of her neck.

"Brandy…" he breathed heavily, showering her with kisses, feeling the rise of her soft bosom against his lips. Wrapping his strong arms about her, they spun melded together, until he had her backed against the kitchen island. Snaking his hot hands down her sides, he grasped her thighs. Lifting her in one smooth motion, he swiftly set her atop the tiled surface.

"Oh!" Brandy tore her lips from his and stared wide-eyed into his drugged gaze.

"What?" he asked impatiently, pressing a hand at the back of her head to draw her in for another kiss. He had her right where he wanted her, perfect height, legs apart, the inn vacant of guests… *Nothing* was going to stop him now.

Flattening a hand to his damp shirt, Brandy held him off. "You just tossed me into one of my just-baked—*hot*—pumpkin pies." And she was well aware she had set them on the *opposite* end of the island only minutes ago.

Dante blinked. He looked down between her legs, saw nothing but that nice V of hers, then leaned around to see her luscious little hind end, indeed, planted firmly into an orange custard pie.

Both of their heads snapped around when a husky roar came from the dining area, accompanied by a tiny baby giggle. "You always were a good aim, brother," Julie chuckled, Kyle perched on her thin hip mimicking his mother's laughter. "He was the quarterback in college, ya know," she said conversationally as she sashayed into the kitchen.

Brandy's face flushed instantly. With a choked cry of mortification, she shoved Dante aside and jumped from the countertop, pulling pie and pan with her.

"Here, let me help," Dante offered, reaching for the pie plate that was clinging to her rear.

Smacking his hand sharply, Brandy backed away. "No! I can…get it myself," she insisted, reaching behind her. With somewhat of a suction tone, and a tiny measure of strength, Brandy pulled the pie from her tail end.

"Hmm," Dante rubbed the stubble on his chin as he cocked his head to study the creamy mess on her backside. "I have a sudden yen for some pumpkin pie…"

Julie tossed her balding head back with raucous laughter. *Yes, things were going to work out just fine*, Julie thought before offering, "Maybe Kyle and I should have our Thanksgiving dinner upstairs in our suite. Give you two time to—er, get out the whipped cream."

Dante grinned roguishly in agreement with his sister. "Brandy, allow me to introduce Julie Saxon, my sister."

Brandy suppressed utter mortification, vaguely studying the gaunt, gray-toned woman. Backing slowly from the room, she replied, "Glad to finally meet you." With a wry, flushed smile, she added, "I would shake your hand, but…"

Julie grinned, her bluish lips thinning. "That orangish tone becomes you."

Brandy continued to back from the room. "I…I'll be right back." In a cautious sprint, she zipped out into the lobby and went regally to her quarters, holding the pie remnants carefully against her derriere with a dishtowel.

CHAPTER 5

He must've shot upstairs for a quick shower during her absence. Looking entirely too virile in the faded denim button-up shirt and his trademark Levis, Brandy watched as he stirred the gravy she'd made. From a rear view, he could've passed as a sexy jeans ad model with his stark black hair falling in wisps around his collar and the snug fit of denim over tight glutes. It was enough to make any woman's heart race.

At the sound of her tiny sigh, Dante turned from the stove. A low whistle erupted from deep within his throat. "Whoa! Brandy, darling, you look…extremely dangerous."

The black leather pants were ironically elegant, yet tight enough to reveal every curve, every valley. She wore a simple white—snug—turtleneck under a black leather blazer. Height was added by three-inch heels. Her hair, pulled back in an artistic mass at the back of her head, was the final clincher. His fingers itched to pull the clip from the silky swirl again, inhale the scent of honey, watch it—hell, *feel* it—as the tresses cascaded over his hands, his face, her bare back…

"Brandy, dear," Julie said from behind her. "You look absolutely fetching. A girl after my own heart." Shakily toting Kyle across the room, she went on, "I just love leather. I was a biker girl for awhile in my wild, wild past."

"T-thank you—I think," Brandy replied curtly, watching as Julie secured Kyle in the highchair, then sat next to him.

Dante poured the steaming gravy into the gravy boat and brought it to the dinner table, placing it next to the mashed potatoes and carved turkey perched on a platter. "Dinner's served," he mocked, bowing and pulling out a chair for her at the head of the table.

"You shouldn't have done all this, Dante," she lowered herself into the chair averting her gaze from those sizzling embers of his as he ever-so-discreetly shimmied his hand down her spine.

"Why not?" he drawled, winking at her as he slid into the chair at her right. "I was anxious and worked up an appetite."

"Yes. Shoveling's very strenuous," Brandy commented, wandering how all that snow had remained intact with him so near. Ignoring the obvious meaning of his words—and the continued tingling at his previous touch—she deliberately studied the candles he'd lit gracing the centerpiece. "Thanks for all your help. I'll discount your room for the service."

"Nonsense," Julie flung a bony hand in the air. Kyle was seated at Brandy's left, Julie strangely sitting further down that side of the table, as if to purposely alienate herself. "Dante was only blowing off steam. Believe me, he wasn't doing anyone any favors."

Dante clasped his hands over his plate with his elbows set on either side. With a grim smile, he held Julie's gaze and said tightly, "My sister has always been a rather blunt, anti-social person."

"It's okay," Brandy glanced from right to left, the sudden tension thick before her very eyes. "I don't care what his reasons were for shoveling the snow. I'm grateful. With my staff out, I would've been out there doing it myself."

Kyle chose that moment to contribute. From his throne in the highchair, he slapped his chubby hands onto the tray. "Num-num, num-num," he demanded.

All eyes turned to him as the mild turmoil in the room evaporated.

"You always want num-num." Dante rolled his eyes, plopping a heaping of mashed potatoes onto his own plate and passing the bowl to Brandy.

Brandy blinked, staring at the bowl without taking it. "Aren't we going to say grace?"

Dante lowered the steaming potatoes slowly and chanced a glance at Julie. "Julie and I aren't…the religious type. We don't make a habit of praying."

Incredulously, Brandy asked, "Why not?"

"We were too busy surviving." Julie speared a slice of turkey with her fork and cut up several tiny pieces, placing them directly on Kyle's tray. Without pause, he tore into the meat.

"Surviving?"

Dante sighed heavily, lifting the bowl once again and forcing Brandy to receive the warm ceramic dish. "Praying never got us anywhere."

Brandy hesitantly spooned a small portion of potatoes onto her plate, smashing the top to make a basin for the gravy before passing it over Kyle and down the length of the table to Julie. "I…I don't understand."

"Dante and I lived on the streets when we were children," Julie threw out, a resentful tone lacing her crackling voice as she accepted the dish.

"Julie, that's enough. She doesn't need details." Dante poured a puddle of gravy over his potatoes before shooting her a warning scowl. No one needed to hear the horror and shame of it, he grumbled silently to himself.

"Believe me," she ignored her brother and barreled on. "We tried everything, including praying, to make our situation better. Nothing worked."

Brandy reached for the gravy, pausing ever-so-briefly as she conjured up images of a young boy and girl, grubby, hungry, cold…alone. A swift wave of compassion engulfed her, for she knew what it was to be lonely, though cold and starving, she gratefully had never had to experience.

Her eyes met Dante's over the dish as he passed it to her. "Oh my gosh," she dragged in a breath to stop the tears. "I'm so sorry you two had to go through that."

"We survived," he shrugged, toyed with the food on his plate.

"Well that certainly calls for a prayer." Pouring a small pond onto her potatoes, she said softly, "Thank you, Lord, for this feast, for the warm roof over our heads, and for the blessing of lovely company on this Thanksgiving Day. Amen."

The room went still, the only sound that of the eerie whistling of the blustery winds outside. Even little Kyle ceased his barbarous feeding activities to gawk at his hostess.

Dante had never heard such a profound statement in his life, had never seen such gentle clarity in eyes so beautifully mint green. The tenderness in her voice still echoed in his head. With a smile of gratitude, he teased, "I think she said grace after all."

Kyle, dispensing anxiously with the uncomfortably tender moment, stretched across his tray reaching unsuccessfully for the bowl of potatoes that his mother had failed to add to the mess in front of him. "Ta-toes! Ta-toes!"

Brandy had found herself lost in the warm gold light of Dante's eyes, enhanced by the flickering candlelight. Tearing her gaze from his, she giggled and reached for the potatoes. "You're a hungry little guy, aren't you?" Plopping a pile of mashed potatoes on his tray, she watched in horror as he dug his chubby little hands into the warm creamy mess, and proceeded to lick his fingers.

"Okay, well, at least someone likes my cooking," she suppressed another giggle.

Julie laughed throatily. "Kyle's going to be just as much of a savage as his uncle."

Dante passed the green beans, then the basket of rolls. Jabbing a buttery, piping-hot roll across the table at Julie, he said, "This coming from a woman who drinks straight from the milk jug?"

Brandy gaped at her female guest. "Really? Well, then, I'll just have to keep the refrigerator under lock and key."

"Bee-bees!" Kyle indicated the green beans with a potato-disguised finger as Julie spooned a pile before him. "Fank-ooh," he expressed his appreciation.

Brandy watched with endearing interest as he did a pincer grasp on one green bean, then proceeded to split it lengthwise and pluck the beans from within the pod. His eyes, so strikingly pale blue against the golden skin, glanced up to study her as he popped the tiny morsels into his mouth. Time stood still. Her heart flipped,-flopped, then ceased to beat as he smiled sweetly at her, his rosy lips spreading across a face smudged with mashed potatoes.

"How old is he?" Brandy's breath hitched. Receiving a corn cob from Dante, she slowly began sampling her plate, her eyes wandering to Kyle now and again.

"He'll be two in May," Julie offered as she picked at the meager portions on her plate.

"Two years, hum," Brandy nodded as she sipped her wine. "Oh, we—that is, Ian and I—moved here two years ago this May to begin refurbishing the inn."

It was at that precise moment that Kyle chose to chime in, "Da-Da!"

Brandy lowered her fluted wine glass slowly as Dante's fork halted midway to his mouth. Her gaze swung to the toddler, her eyes meeting his. Blue, blue eyes the color of crystal clear tropical waters, the same color, the same shape as...

Dante cleared his throat explosively, then stood, scooting his chair noisily on the wooden floor. "So, got anymore of that pumpkin pie?"

Julie glanced from Brandy, whose mouth was now hanging open in an O as her eyes began to widen considerably, to her brother. "Dante, it's time."

Brandy disengaged her eyes from Kyle's. Looking from Dante, as he stood there like a tiger ready to spring across the table, to Julie, who resembled a stubborn ghost, a feeling of dread slammed into her.

Just what was going on here? she wondered as her pulse slammed thickly in her throat.

Julie glanced up into the defiant eyes of her brother. "Dante, I don't have much time left, and you know it. It's time."

Brandy sat motionless like a trapped rabbit just waiting for the gunshot through her sleek fur. What was this all about? Something was extremely odd here…

"Time for what?" Brandy stood and pinned Dante with a molten stare.

Dante reached for her, then held his hands up in surrender as she shoved them away. "Julie, tell me what's going on…*now?*" she demanded, swinging her baffled gaze to the sickly woman.

Julie got shakily to her feet. Oh shit, she thought, as waves of dizziness washed over her and Ian's illuminated image began to float before her. *Go away,* she silently urged him, her vision blurring. *She deserves the truth, Ian!*

Raising a trembling hand, she swatted his ghostly form from the air, her eyelids getting heavier with each ounce of energy she expended. She'd been certain this was the right thing to do, but glancing once again at Brandy, she wondered if Ian weren't right. Thrown off guard by the confusion she now saw in Brandy's eyes, she hesitated. For years she'd taken second to this woman, even hated her for a time, but had grown used to the idea of having a part-time man around the house. She'd loved having time to herself, treasuring the days when she could sit for hours with her infant sleeping soundly next to her as she devoured any book she could get her hands on. Making up for lost time, for all those years she'd been denied an education, and yes, for those horrid years she'd ran wild and did what she had to survive, she'd taught herself about the wonders of the world and life itself.

Well, now her life was getting down to the wire, and this was one of her final plans to iron out. Her son came first. She would put him ahead of Dante and his attempt to control the situation, before herself, and yes, before the pain she would inflict on this woman who'd been Ian's wife, but whom Julie had grown to like in such a short time. And I'll most certainly, she thought with renewed vigor as she narrowed her eyes on Ian's spirit, put him before you, Ian.

"Well?" Brandy urged, alarm rising in her as each second ticked by.

"Kyle's—" Julie swayed as her face went chalk-white.

"Julie!" Dante raced around the table to lower her into a chair. Reaching for a glass of water, he held it to her lips. "Here, drink this."

She took a meager sip, then shoved the glass aside. "Kyle. He's…" she stammered and her head began to bob from side-to-side, her vision fading in and out as Ian's apparition surrounded her.

Brandy gasped and came to Julie's other side. "Julie, are you okay? Should I call an ambulance?"

Her head rolled back to rest on her brother's shoulder as he lifted her effortlessly into his arms. "No…no ambulance. There's nothing they can…do anymore. Just need to rest," she whispered hoarsely.

Dante studied Brandy's compassionate expression as he backed away from her with his limp sister in his arms. "Could you finish feeding Kyle? I'll be down soon to get him."

"Of course," Brandy agreed, glancing at the tot as he scooped food into his mouth, oblivious to the commotion going on around him.

With her acceptance, Dante raced from the room and up the stairs.

Lowering herself to the chair where Julie had left her barely-touched meal, Brandy muttered, "Mommy's going to be just fine, honey."

"Ma-ma!" Kyle reached for her with outstretched arms. His entire shirtfront was splattered with corn stuck in dried potatoes, and a lone kernel sat directly on the tip of his nose.

Her heart melting once again, she looked through the creamy mess of his pudgy face into those eyes again, eyes the same shape and color as...Ian's? No. It couldn't be, she laughed nervously. It was impossible. She was jumping to conclusions, loosing her mind quite completely.

"No, sweetie, I'm not Ma-ma." Reaching for a linen napkin, she dipped it in Julie's glass of water and proceeded to unbury Kyle from his own self-destruction. Before she could wipe his last hand, he balled a fist and rubbed his drooping eyes, adding white-tipped globs to his lashes. "Oh, don't do that, honey." Brandy suppressed a grin, and he squirmed while she attempted to remove the muddle from his eyes.

Clucking, she untied his bib and dropped the soaked terry cloth onto the highchair table. "You're going to have to be completely stripped," she said softly, unstrapping him and standing him in the highchair long enough to wipe the remnants from his pants.

He held both arms up to her, and in that moment, she felt her maternal hormones race. So this was what she'd been missing. This was what the doctor hadn't warned her of, what it meant to be infertile, to never experience with her own offspring, the aching need to nurture and love.

Reaching for the little bundle, she tucked him against her breast and sighed simultaneously with him as he laid his sleepy head on her shoulder. In seconds, she could hear his light even breathing, could feel the soft innocence of him relaxing heavily, trustingly against her. Inhaling, she closed her eyes as the scent of powder and warm baby, all gently assaulted her senses. Taking cautious steps, she crossed to the window and pushed aside the gauzy Priscilla curtains.

Outside, the sky was darkening to a dismal gray. Snow was falling in swirling fat flakes as the wind whipped under the eaves, playing an eerie musical tune. Brandy swayed, humming, holding the toddler safely against her as nature unearthed its wrath once again on her inn. But now, at this very moment, she savored the solace, was grateful to be here alone with this pure yet mischievous child that had a mother who was very ill, and an uncle that had taken a leave of absence from his own life to bring his dying sister and her son to a place of peace…her bed and breakfast. A place that, as far as she was concerned, had no vacancy at this moment.

Hugging Kyle closer, she looked down at the dark lashes fanned over round cheeks. He was completely at peace in her arms, unaware that he may soon be motherless, or even that he should be praying for Julie's survival. Survival. Julie had said they'd done what they had to survive on the streets as children. Now, looking at this innocent child in her arms, her heart began to crack and break as she pictured Kyle being forced to sustain the same unthinkable ordeal in order to breathe, eat, stay warm, be loved…

It was there that he found her, framed by the window and the dim sky outside, holding his nephew as lovingly as any mother would. She was humming softly to him, caressing his back, kissing the top of his dark, potato-crusted hair. As she swayed, he watched her body take on that maternal stance that only a woman, only a mother, could. She was beautiful, breathtaking, and somehow, the sight of her gently caring for Kyle, a child she barely knew, sent a swift surge to his loins.

He heard her murmur to the sleeping child, "Your ma-ma's gonna be just fine," as she shifted him to the other shoulder.

"You're very good at that," Dante came up behind her and wrapped his arms around the woman and child.

The feeling of completeness engulfed her as she was surrounded by his warmth. "He's an adorable child. Is Julie all right?"

He raced his hands up her arms. "She's exhausted. I put her to bed."

Staring out at the darkening day, Brandy said sadly, "She doesn't have much longer, does she?"

"No." The one simple word was filled with emotion, and she felt him sigh heavily against her.

"How long?" she whispered.

"Three, four weeks tops. Chemo, radiation, surgery, all failed to get the cancer. It's spread to her lymph nodes." She heard him smile. "Her vanity went with the mastectomy. That, to her, was worse than dying."

"I'm sorry she—you've all had to go through this ordeal. If I can do anything…"

"You've done enough putting up with us here for the last few weeks."

She leaned her head back against his shoulder. "Stay as long as you like."

His arms tightened about her and the child. "Soon. Soon, we'll be out of your hair." He kissed her temple, taking comfort in how right it felt to hold her, justifying the words he would speak before the night was over. God, how to tell her the truth?

Brandy closed her eyes, savoring the feel of innocent child at her breast, and powerfully attractive man at her back.

It was time, Dante thought as he felt her sway against him again. Julie was right. They couldn't continue to stay here indefinitely without giving her an explanation. She'd find out eventually anyway, and the longer he dragged it out, the harder it would be on them all.

Tell her, you fool, he scolded himself. *You can't wait any longer.*

She felt him tense and his arms fell from her. Turning, she asked alarmed, "Dante, what is it?"

He swallowed a massive lump, then studied her lovely features, now drawn in alarm. "I'll be back," he evaded, plucking Kyle from her embrace. "As soon as I get him to bed, I'll come and explain everything to you."

"Everything...?"

She watched him go, watched helplessly as he strolled from the dining room with the ebony-haired child tucked comfortably upon his shoulder. She felt the emptiness of her arms as he disappeared from view, and she knew a dread worse than impending death itself.

CHAPTER 6

"Brandy!" Dante's breathing was heavy, his face flushed as he pounded on her door. He was psyched up now, ready to rid himself of this terrible secret that was eating him alive.

When she finally pulled the door slowly open, he was leaning roguishly against the doorjamb, one shoulder supporting him, his hands stuffed in the pockets of his jeans, and a brown leather binder tucked against his side. Stepping passed her, he chided gently, "You were supposed to wait in the kitchen for me."

"I..." she studied his back as he stepped around her and went down the hall. "I waited...a long time."

"Sorry," he scanned the living room, took in the roaring fire, the soft feminine touches of wicker and downy pillows, all so very Brandy. "I had to bathe Kyle," he explained.

She'd pulled a mattress before the fireplace, he noted, blankets piled there as if she'd made it her permanent bed. Had it been loneliness that'd drawn her away from the bedroom, an effort to distance herself from the room she and Ian had occasionally shared? Or was it the need for the fire's substitute warmth that only loving arms could truly provide?

"Would you like a drink?" she asked, once again playing the accommodating hostess. Crossing to a side table, she made the decision for him, pouring him a splash of whiskey in a crystal tumbler.

Immediately she mixed herself a margarita, and downed half of it in one swallow, then slammed the cup upon the pine surface. She was going to need every bit of calming assistance she could get, she was sure of it.

"Thank you," he said when she glided across the room to press the glass in his hand. Guiltily, he noted the trembling of her hand as it brushed his, could feel the frightened coolness of it.

She nodded her response, then went to sit upon the mattress, curling her legs under her as she studied the leaping flames.

"I apologize, Brandy, for putting you through all this, and on a holiday at that. If I wasn't such a damn coward, we would've had this talk much sooner."

"What? Is this confessional?" she asked weakly, dreading his next words.

Dante stepped slowly toward her, depositing the portfolio on the nearest table. Looking down into the glazed worry of her eyes, he saw the flames of the fire reflecting against the glassy orbs, nakedly exposing her emotions. Tossing the whiskey back in one swallow, he divulged of the tumbler and dropped down on the mattress next to her. Raising a hand to tuck a stray tendril behind her ear, he ignored the subtle flinch and replied, "Brandy, I don't want to hurt you, but…there's so much to tell you. And God help me, if I could change it, I would."

Brandy groaned. "Would you just get on with it? Please," she begged, her eyes shimmering with sudden tears. "I can't take any more suspense."

A tenderness welled up in him, and he felt his chest tighten. This woman, this innocent bystander, was at his mercy. He'd known about the affair all along, had let it happen, and had done nothing to alleviate Brandy's oblivion to it. But now was the time to lay all the factors out before her, to open her eyes and let her see what she was going to be walking into, what she'd already been in the middle of without a clue.

"Brandy," he reached for her, pulling her into the circle of his arms. When he finally spoke, his voice broke, and he murmured, "I'll explain everything, I promise...but first..."

Brandy felt the strength of his arms as they came around her, shuddered as he began to plant soft, fluttery kisses all over her face. In spite of her determination to resist, she nearly collapsed in his embrace, much as she had that nasty, rainy day of Ian's funeral. Gripping the front of his shirt, she tipped her head back, speared his pained eyes with her own, and whispered, "Just...get it over with. *Please!*"

His hands slid up her stiff back and came around to cup her jaw. Those lips, those fabulous heart-shaped lips, quivered under his scrutiny, and he found himself distracted, starving for the taste of them.

"Oh, babe..." he whispered huskily, dipping his head to press his warm lips against hers, stilling them until they stiffened, hesitated, relaxed, yielded. She tasted so sweet, a cool margarita sweetness. *Just a few more moments,* he thought as he deepened the kiss. *Just a bit longer to savor you before you cast me out of your life.*

Brandy wasn't quite sure why she allowed it. Maybe she just didn't want to hear words that she sensed would change things between them. Was she grasping at something she felt may slip away if he spoke his secrets? Or had she mixed the drink too strong? Not until later would she realize it had nothing to do with alcohol. Her answer was more potent than any drug, any cocktail: Dante. Dante and the powerful passion he dangled before her, tempting her with the fierce, sleek mastery of the genuine feeling in his eyes, his arms, his aura.

She didn't want to discuss Ian and his business secrets. Hell, she didn't want to ever discuss Ian again. She wanted this...

The kiss intensified, drawing her into another dimension of pure need and raw urgency. When one hand slid gently, firmly to her back, pressing her full against him, Brandy knew she'd lost the battle of principal she'd been armed to fight. Ian, Julie, even little Kyle, all faded from her thoughts as this man, this magnificent specimen, swept her up into a whirlwind of need that slammed into her with a force as merciless, and yet as forgiving, as nature.

"Darling, you're so…" he lowered his head, inhaling the soft fragrance of her, flickering his tongue as he made his way to the top of her turtleneck. "So stunning. Please," he begged as the hand at her jaw fell to cup, squeeze, massage one ample breast. "Please. Let me make love to you."

His words were more of an aphrodisiac than his flaming hands. "Dante…" She whispered breathlessly. "I—I…it's crazy, but, yes. Yes. Please…make love to me."

In one swift motion, the floodgates were opened wide; he removed her hair clip and fell with her to the mattress before the fire. Racing his hands up her shirt and divulging of it expertly, he flung it onto the sofa. She wore a white lacy bra that supported her swelling bosom, and he released it in one snap, watching with fascination as her breasts fell ever-so-slightly, the nipples growing tight with his hot inspection.

She was pure femininity with her disheveled gold hair fanned out around her, and her bosom heaving upward with breathless passion. Eyes slanting cat-like, she beckoned to him, reaching down to unfasten her own leather pants. He surveyed her, animal-like, as his mate accommodated him, raising her slim hips to shed the barrier. His eyes skimmed her, memorized every valley and plane where her chest gently tapered to a narrow ribcage, and her flat belly quivered in anticipation above the trim golden triangle between her legs

On an inward hiss, Dante unbuttoned his shirt and tossed it aside, "You're exquisite, Brandy. The most gorgeous, sexy woman…"

In response, she raised her slim arms, welcoming him into her heart, one leg slightly bent in that last-ditch effort to hold him at bay, yet beckon with inborn seductive charms. She watched impatiently, amazed at the throbbing between her legs, as he stood and removed his jeans. It was then, when her eyes went from the ruggedly handsome face, down over the sculpted chest and washboard abdomen, to the glorious core of his manhood, that she knew she was lost to him forever. Every inch of him stood ready for her, for the lovemaking that she was powerless to stop—didn't want to stop! And when he came to her, stretched his warm length against her bare skin, she felt herself being enveloped in the fire of him, and knew a blissfulness that was more gratifying than the act of love itself.

But she wasn't to let it end there. Their eyes met, locking helplessly together, as she cupped his darkly whiskered jaw, his ebony hair falling around his face like an angelic demon. He turned his lips into her hand, planting a butterfly kiss in the palm, then she pressed her hand to that hard chest, making a hot trail from breast to shoulder to tight bicep. Keeping him imprisoned with the heat of her gaze, she returned to his chest and slowly lowered her hand to his flat stomach, down over his hip, then lower, until she imprisoned him with her hot palm. Velvety smooth, she marveled at the hardness, the massive size of him, encircling his steel manhood with her hand, stroking.

"Christ—Brandy," Dante warned, hissing between clenched teeth as he pulled her gently free of him. "No. I want to be inside you when I..."

Even as he forced her thighs apart with his hips, she said huskily, locking her arms around his neck, "Then come to me. Make me forget..."

It was a challenge that somehow gave him great pride. She was turning her heart over to him, wrenching it from widowhood as she did so, something she should have done months ago. But he refused to think of her circumstances which painfully entwined with his own—hell, couldn't think, not with her eyes glassy with passion as she spread her legs in welcoming invitation.

The flames of the fire flickered, and a draft of ice-cold air whooshed down the chimney. Ashes rose and fluttered over the lovers, neither aware that the protective barrier of love they were building around themselves was the one dose of water that put the smoldering ashes out, that kept Ian from wrenching them apart. Even in the dimension of purgatory where his spirit hovered insanely between life and eternal peace, he had powers that inflamed his immortal ego. But at that moment, he felt a swift surge of helpless anger as he watched his wife and best friend become lovers. Unable to witness the one thing that he'd never planned, and seeing that he was powerless to pry them apart, he reluctantly rose through the ceiling and settled himself around Julie and his son—but not before sending a potted plant crashing to the floor.

Oblivious to the chill in the air and the noises of an irate ghost, the lovers carried on, exploring, whispering soothing words of passion to one another.

Dante lowered his mouth to hers, seeing the glittering tears of passion form in her eyes. As he gently probed her silky mouth with his tongue, so did he with his shaft, slowly encasing it with the tight, sleekness of her womanhood. She cried out, arching her back as her moan erupted deeply into his mouth.

"Dante…" she panted, showering his lips with tender kisses as she stilled her hips.

"Yes, baby," he breathed, pulling his lips free to capture her glazed, burning eyes with his own. Lord, but she felt like sweet heaven! he thought as she remained painfully still.

Suddenly, she shifted, pressing him away, and came over him, straddling him like a stallion.

"Now," she cried, slowly impaling herself with him. "Now…" she whispered huskily.

It was all the encouragement he needed. Thrusting his hips, he rose to meet her, stroking himself deeper inside her. Gripping her hair, he yanked her down until his lips captured hers, exploring every inch of her. When she gasped, moaned, fell upon his chest, he felt his blood quicken, his heart thudding heavily against his breastbone. Her hands slid over his trim sides, reaching down to grasp his buttocks, slamming him tighter into her. She closed her eyes as the fever built, then rose straight upon him, riding, reaching, soaring into a world of white-hot passion. Her hands fluttered up her own flat belly, over her glistening full breasts, and up to tangle in her hair. And when he called out her name, she opened her eyes, locking them with his fiery ones as his hands stroked up her torso. She threw her head back in response, howling like the she-wolf he'd transformed her into.

They exploded together at that moment, a strange mix of raw, bare emotion mirrored in each other's souls. Then she collapsed upon him in exhaustion, and they quietly drifted into a world where neither would have to analyze what had just passed between them.

He came awake some time in the chilly early hours of the morning, shifting lazily as he felt the soft hair brush his cheek. He didn't want to think of the portfolio. That would come soon enough. But now, now was a time to savor her, to remember how they'd made love through the night, how she'd cried out his name and welcomed him with a breathless abandon. She was an amazing woman, and he still marveled at Ian's stupidity—and his own.

What was he to do now? He had succeeded in entangling his life further, and complicating hers beyond repair.

They were still lying on the mattress before the hearth, blankets tangled haphazardly around their naked bodies. He inhaled the scent of her mingled with their lovemaking. And he watched with keen interest as Brandy stirred, the sheet falling from her chest to reveal luscious full breasts, soft, pink-tipped.

"Brandy," he nudged her nipple with a soft kiss. Instantly, it sprang to life, begging for his touch. "Wake up, Sleeping Beauty."

Her eyes fluttered, twin orbs of fuzzy green. "Dante?" she asked, as if she hadn't known he'd been with her through the night. But she'd known, known with all her heart that he'd been there. And how very happy she was to wake and see his devastatingly handsome face first thing in the morning!

He pulled her tightly against his side. "I have to say it now. I can't stand to keep it from you any longer."

The tone, and the direction of his words, woke her like thick caffeine-laced coffee. Taking a deep cleansing breath, she whispered, "Okay. Go ahead." Go ahead and ruin it all, she thought grimly.

Dante tucked her head under his chin, aware that she would bolt from him as soon as the words were out of his mouth. His arms came around her clamping her to him.

Sighing warily, he blurted out, "Kyle is Ian's son."

There was a long pause where she neither stiffened nor spoke. Then, as if all hell had broken loose, she was flailing her arms, kicking against him and the blankets, scrambling to her feet.

Arms akimbo, she shrieked, "*What?*".

Dante looked up at her in all her naked glory, hair in disarray about her shoulders, slender hips and luscious bosom. She was like a naked angel—and God help the direction of his thoughts!

"His son…" tears glittered in her eyes as she gulped down a painful lump, then sailed nude from the room. Within seconds, she returned, wrapped in the white robe.

He was wearing only his Levis and bent before the hearth rebuilding the fire until it sparked to a renewed blaze. She paused in arrest at the image he made against the inferno, stoking her own flames deep within her womb, recalling with crystal-clear clarity, the feel of those rippling, corded muscles under her hands. Recalling, for she knew she'd never feel them firsthand again.

He turned and swept her with a searing gaze. It was that white sheer robe again, he thought, his muscles tensing as he recalled the way she'd felt against him when he'd cornered her in the office weeks ago, the way her nipples had strained against the slick fabric.

"Brandy," he returned to the mattress, fell warily upon it. "I know this is a shock—"

"A shock!" she shrieked. "You son of a bitch!" Kicking the blankets that were wadded up at his feet, she seethed, "Get out."

When he only laid there looking up at her in all his half-naked, tempting glory, she leaned down and singed him with a boiling gaze. "Are you deaf? *I—said—get—out!*"

"Brandy, I'm so sorry," he held up his hands in defense. "I knew all along about...the affair...that you didn't know about Kyle. But you've got to understand, I didn't know you at all. Even so, I did feel a need to come to you, to confess everything to you. But..." he glanced away, throwing an arm over his brow, "I was a coward. I couldn't bring myself to hurt you. And I used my loyalty to my sister, and somewhat to Ian, as an excuse to remain mute."

Feeling a sudden urge to smack him, she caught sight of the forgotten portfolio lying mockingly on the coffee table. Plucking it up, she jabbed it toward him instead. "Is this more? Is this what I'd suspected? He sold my inn?"

"Brandy."

"Out with it, cad," she spat, grinding her teeth together and tossing the leather binder at him. It arrived on target, right into his crotch.

Dante jolted, then moaned, sitting upright to clutch himself where she'd given him a terrible blow. "Jesus, Brandy," he groaned.

"Jesus, *Brandy*?" she hissed. "You deserved that. And to think, I even *slept* with you," she nearly shuddered. "You hid from me that your sister was my husband's mistress, that her infant son was *my* husband's son, and all the while, you're *living under my roof!*"

He couldn't argue with one word. Blinking, he croaked, "We paid for our room."

"Ooohh!" her brows came down to crush her blazing eyes. "You pathetic," she kicked the mattress, "idiotic," she kicked it again, "*loser!*"

Dante flinched, then rose like a provoked Adonis prepared to finally fight back. "I may be pathetic and idiotic," he straightened, his chest swelling, "but I'm no loser."

She took a step back and her eyes grazed the hard, sculpted length of him, falling briefly to where his jeans gaped open where he'd neglected to zip them. Jutting her chin toward the portfolio, she spat, "Then get on with it. Show me the documents so I can start packing."

With a heavy sigh, he plucked up the binder, then fell to the sofa and patted the seat near him. Brandy crossed her arms over her chest and went to stand at his side, refusing to sit down near him.

She had every right, Dante knew, to react this way. But still, it galled him that she was taking it out on him, punishing him for her husband's choices. Never mind the fact that he'd known all along, that he'd brought his sister and nephew here to dangle under her nose. That choice had been his, but he wasn't quite prepared, given that they'd become lovers, to accept his mistakes.

All he knew was there'd been something so very right in the way she'd felt in his arms, beneath him, in his heart…

"Well?" she fumed, waiting rigidly at his side.

Setting it on the table before him, he flipped open the leather case. Leafing through, he stopped somewhere in the middle of a stack of documents.

Glancing up, he studied her delicate profile. "This is Ian's last will and testament. As his lawyer, I'm the only one who knew of it—except Julie—or who had access to it."

Of course 'except Julie,' she thought darkly. And *she* had been his wife, not Julie! What was wrong with this picture? she seethed inwardly. Lowering herself reluctantly next to him, she lifted the binder onto her lap.

Under her shaky breath, she focused on the document and read, "I, Ian Joseph MacKay, do hereby leave this, my last will…"

Suddenly, she pushed it aside, dropping it into Dante's lap. "I can't read it. You read it to me."

Snapping the folder shut, Dante said, "I don't need to read it. I know it by heart."

"Give me a quick summary," she hissed, her mouth tasting foul and bitter.

He leaned back against the cushion and turned to face her. "Are you sure?"

"Dante…" she warned, her expression glittering with warning.

"Okay." Reaching for her hand, he entwined his fingers with hers, gripping tightly as she struggled to free her hand. "It's his will, as stated. Ian died broke—except for your inn. But he left half of it to…Julie."

There was a long silence as his words soaked in.

"*What?*" Brandy screeched, snatching her hand so quickly from his, he cringed from the hot friction of it.

Dante leaned forward, placed his elbows on his knees, and held his throbbing head in his hands. "You heard me. He left half the inn to Julie."

Tears of anger engorged her eyes. Wiping them furiously away, she shot to her feet, raising a hand toward the door. "Get out. *Get out!*"

"Brandy, I—"

Slamming her hands onto her narrow hips, she bent to his eye level, affording him a provocative peek of her cleavage. "You pack your sister and that baby up and *get out of* my *inn!*"

He hesitated for a split second, then rose to stand menacingly before her, his arms akimbo as well. "No," he said simply.

Lowering her hands to tight fists at her sides, she snarled, "She will not get half of what I've worked so hard for. She was just his mistress, for God's sake. I was his *wife!*"

Raising a hand to massage his own aching neck, Dante sighed, "She's dying, Brandy. Ian knew it when he bought this place. He knew you'd keep it afloat, and that it was the only legacy he had for

Kyle. He left it to Kyle, actually, through Julie…hers until she…passes away. And I will not move her when she's…so close."

Oh, man, he couldn't have made her feel any tinier. Lowering herself shakily onto the sofa, she uttered, "So I'm to share the inn with his illegitimate son."

"No, Brandy. All the hard work is yours to be rewarded. I'll work out a deal with you, to deposit a percentage of the net profits, say ten—twenty percent, into an account for him. He has a right to his inheritance, whether you or I think it's fair. But you won't have to share the space with him. I'll be raising him in Chicago, after she—"

"I'll have my lawyer get in touch with you," she cut in, propping her feet onto the coffee table next to the packet of damning papers, the valuable inheritance, she snorted, that her beloved husband had left her.

His gaze followed the shapely calf from ankle to knee. "Brandy…I'm so sorry. I—"

Raising a palm to him, she stared straight ahead into the crackling fire he'd just stoked. "Please. Don't. Just go."

And he did. Taking one last, longing look at the cozy bed they'd shared before the fire, and the woman who'd somehow entwined herself throughout his soul, he quietly left her quarters and returned to his nursemaid duties to his sister and nephew.

She sat there for an eternity, staring into the dying flames. Her gaze dropped to the bed laid out before the fire like a stage. Dante had come here to do this, to shatter her dreams, before she'd become entangled in his dark eroticism. He'd duped her, used her, gotten what he'd craved from her first, because, slimy lawyer that he was, he'd known that she'd never have slept with him if he'd revealed his deception first. Clutching the robe against her trembling chest, she rose and walked rigidly from the room.

Ian—that bastard—even from his chilly grave, she thought as she walked to the kitchen, had seen to everything. Even his wife's seduction by his supposed friend.

A sudden wind whipped through her hair and she heard the stereo turn itself on in the living room.

"Go to hell, Ian!" she flipped him the bird, grinding her teeth together. "And get the hell out of my house!"

The wind died. The music faded.

"Bastard," she hissed, pouring water in the coffee pot and setting it to brew.

The machine began to perk, come to life, steam.

"Dante had better get the hell out of here," she warned aloud as she held a mug under the hot stream of coffee. When her cup was full, she went to sit at the narrow breakfast bar. The last thing she needed, she mused bitterly, was to lay awake at night and hear Ian's son crying in the suite above her.

You're dead now, Ian. You're never going to mess with my life again, she thought darkly, as her head fell heavily to the bar.

Another gust rustled her hair and stirred the flames in the next room.

"Get the hell out of my life!" she shouted, lifting her head in defiant defense, fisting her hands next to the mug.

The wind ceased immediately. The room was still, save for the cheerful perk of the coffee pot.

Tears came so fiercely, she was helpless to stop them. Sniffling, she carried her cup back to the living room and sat before the withering fire. What was she going to do? Her dead husband's mistress was tucked away in *her* inn, directly above her, and…dying. In addition, there was an innocent child involved, Ian's child.

"Ian," she cried softly, punching the pillow and laying down to curl onto her side. "How could you?"

But Ian, still a coward in his ghostly state, refrained from responding to that one.

Brandy knew precisely how. He'd never had a schedule he could live by. He'd come and gone as he'd pleased—and naïve ditz that she'd been, she'd allowed him to use that revolving door, hell, she'd *trusted* him to use it! But more than anything, she'd chased him away by not providing him with a son, the one thing his mistress had been able to give him.

And now she'd gone and complicated the matter further by becoming involved with the mistress' brother.

Oh, Ian, you wretched, wretched jerk!

CHAPTER 7

"I need to talk to her myself," Julie said gruffly from her place under a pile of quilts. She just couldn't seem to get warm enough, couldn't get enough air into her weak lungs.

"She's had enough for one day, Jules," Dante warned, his hand shooting out to grasp Kyle's leg before he could slither away during the diaper change fiasco. "Kyle. Hold still."

"Kyle!" with some effort, Julie reprimanded her mischievous toddler. "You mind Uncle Dante."

Kyle went still as a mannequin, pivoting only his eyes to search out his stern mother in the bed.

Julie suppressed a grin. "Good boy," she praised. "Dante, take me to her. I *have* to talk to her."

Securing the diaper tape, he slid the wriggly ham legs into the one-piece heavy sleeper. "And what am I supposed to do with this monster when I'm hauling you around?"

Julie's strength, just in the last twenty-four hours, had diminished considerably. Dante had been carrying her back and forth from bed to bathroom all day. But she wasn't allowing that fact to damper her mood. Not when she was certain that Dante had slept with Brandy last night. Where else could he have been with a vacant inn, and the dawn fresh on the horizon when he'd come tiptoeing in this morning?

Julie now considered his question. The wheels in her tired brain turning sluggishly, she thought, *what better way to further seal her plans than to dangle the adorable monster in front of Brandy as often as possible?*

"Bundle him up. I'll take him with me."

Dante snorted. "No way. He'd be a holy terror. And you're not going to be that cruel by flaunting him in front of her."

"He's going with me," Julie demanded hoarsely, suppressing a cough.

Dante bit off his next words. "I assume if I refuse, you'll just do it anyway."

Julie rose unsteadily, flipping the blankets aside. "Damn right."

He sighed resignedly. How the hell could he deny a dying, stubborn woman?

The rear balcony was expansive, with a portion jutting out over the sloping back yard. Beyond the boundaries of the courtyard, beyond the white-washed fence and the tiny frozen creek that sliced through the dells, the estate resembled a huge sea of white foamy waves, cresting here, troughing there. Peering through the firs and maples that speared the crystal blue sky, Brandy could see the crescent-shaped iced-over lake with a glaze that gleamed in the afternoon sun.

Geese flew overhead, their honking squawks echoing across the land. From her place on the wooden glider bench, at the far reaches of the balcony, she squinted against the glare of the sun. It was a chilly day, and she burrowed deeper into her heavy parka, ignoring the white puffs coming from her nostrils, ignoring the cool of the bench permeating her long underwear.

Today's only reservation had canceled. The woman, a writer seeking solace to complete her latest novel, had phoned to inform Boomer that the airport in St. Louis had delayed nearly all flights due to inclement weather. The author's had been canceled altogether, thus lowering Brandy's profits yet again.

What was she to do? The weather had been responsible for a large amount of revenue losses, as well as staffing difficulties. She still needed to pay the mortgage and utilities, make out payroll checks, buy stock for the kitchen. If only Ian hadn't sold the software company...

Pushing her toe against the snow-covered balcony, Brandy swayed against the light breeze, gaining a measure of contentment as the glider squeaked and lulled her into a relaxed swing. She supposed she could ask *them* for help with the mortgage. After all, she snorted to herself, it was half Julie's responsibility. If Julie was going to claim half of the inn for herself, she could claim half the debt.

And there was no doubting it. Brandy had scanned the legal forms after Dante's departure earlier this morning, recognizing Ian's scrawled signature. He'd truly done it. He'd gifted her with a dream, then promptly snatched it from her, even from his grave. The pain of it was more a crusty anger, a festering sore that, time and again, was being wrenched open with the sharpest blade Ian could find. She could swear he was a demon haunting her to no end.

Brandy clenched her jaw. A mistress. What a fool she'd been!

She was expected to share her dream with Ian's mistress—and son. And to further complicate things, she'd gone and slept with the mistress' brother! What had she been thinking?

"If you clamp your jaw any tighter," Julie interrupted her dark thoughts, "you'll need to get dental work."

Brandy stiffened, her gaze swinging sharply. Dante held Julie effortlessly in his arms while she snuggled deep in a downy sleeping bag. His stare was unwavering, boring challengingly into hers. And once again, she was reminded of how she could be so drawn to this man—and how he'd betrayed her.

"What are you doing out here?" she asked both of them, her eyes narrowing to mere slits.

"We need to talk," Julie said frankly. "Put me down, Dante," she ordered her brother.

He obeyed, lowering her gently to the glider. His eyes swept Brandy warily, but he said nothing to her. To Julie, he replied, "Let me know when you've frozen. I'll come back for you." With that, he spun on his booted heel and started across the lawn.

Brandy folded her arms and stared out across the breathtaking land that would probably be foreclosed on within the year. "I have nothing to say to you."

"Hold still!" Julie screeched.

That had Brandy slicing a look at her adversary. "Excuse me?"

Julie giggled weakly, pulling a chubby bundle from the depths of the sleeping bag. "It's Kyle. He's being such a booger today."

Ian's son!

Brandy ignored the flip of her heart as those blue MacKay eyes peeped out at her. They'd been smart, she thought bitterly. They'd hooked her with the child before she'd known who his father was. "It's too cold out here for him," she ripped her gaze from the imp.

"Nonsense. He loves the cold. Can't keep him under his covers at night. He sweats like a piglet."

Brandy cracked a reluctant smile as Kyle slapped his chubby hands together and squealed, "Piggy, piggy!" And in that moment, she saw only his uncle.

Julie turned a gaunt, pale face to Brandy and smiled in return. "He loves Piglet," the wracking cough overtook her as she struggled to speak. "You know, on Winnie the Pooh?"

Yes, she knew. Her brother, Brian, had been nuts about Winnie the Pooh.

"Look, Brandy," Julie sobered, suppressing another cough. "I don't have much time left, so I'm going to get right to the point. Several points, actually."

Brandy reluctantly gave in and pushed them off with her snow boot, sending the glider into a high swing. It wouldn't be proper to shove a feeble dying woman off the balcony, would it? she silently asked herself.

Kyle leered snaggletoothed at her. God, he looked so much like Dante, except…the eyes. "Somehow, I knew you would," Brandy replied frostily, drawing her coat tighter to her breast.

Julie lifted a bony shoulder. "Kyle is my priority. I'm sorry if anything I say hurts you."

Pushing them higher yet, her boot scraping the top layer of snow, Brandy sighed, "Just say it, Julie."

"Ma-ma! Peez. Ma-ma!" Kyle held out his arms to Brandy, his hands, enclosed in his snowsuit, apparently waving his encouragement at her.

Right on cue, little man. Julie lifted him out of the sleeping bag. "He wants you."

Brandy swallowed a huge lump, and her eyes locked with those sky-blue ones that, even now, were looking pitifully at her, like a rejected puppy. "No, no, honey. I'm not Ma-ma."

"He calls all females Ma-ma," Julie said with mock disgust before shoving Kyle onto Brandy's lap. *But one day*, Julie vowed silently, *he'll call only you Ma-ma.* "This is Brandy, Kyle. Brandy," she informed her wriggly son.

"Bran-ma?" he asked, his face scrunching, puzzled.

Julie laughed weakly. "Yes. Bran-ma."

Brandy's arms went around the soft, warm bundle—to prevent him from falling off her lap into the snow, she assured herself. Pulling him tightly against her, he immediately snuggled his head in the crook of her neck.

"He likes you," Julie announced. Swallowing a lump of mixed jealousy and relief, she zipped the sleeping bag up around her chin.

"Yes, he does, doesn't he?" Brandy admitted, closing her eyes briefly to inhale the mixed scent of baby and crisp Wisconsin country air.

"His father is here, you know…" Julie said softly.

"Ian?" Brandy laughed bitterly, petting the tiny back, combing her hands through his downy dark hair. "That's ridiculous. It's just a joke."

"It's true," Julie stared into the sky, her eyes glassy as an eagle soared overhead. "He's come to me...in my fevered dreams. He's angry that you've hooked up with Dante."

"Hooked up?" Brandy choked on her words. She wouldn't quite call it "hooked up"—anymore, at least.

Julie sent her a calming look. "It's okay. I'm plugging for you. Ian will eventually see it my way."

Clearly uncomfortable with the topic of Ian's spirit—for she'd known there was strange energy and forces under her roof, yet she hadn't *truly* believed it was Ian who haunted her inn—she then replied tensely, "I don't know what you're talking about, but if you *are* communicating with him somehow, would you mind giving him a message?"

"Certainly."

"Tell him to go to hell."

Julie paused, speechless for once, then flopped her head back against the glider and let out a deep, rolling fit of laughter. "I told him," she wiped the hysterical tears from her pale face, "the same thing."

Brandy suppressed a grin and continued to snuggle little Kyle's warm body against her.

"Okay, to get back to business," Julie recovered, then leaned heavily into the glider, her eyes drooping with the exhaustion this short outing had already caused her.

"Business," Brandy concurred, her jaw set. "Something I need to get back to shortly myself, before *we* lose everything."

Julie exhaled shakily, a small puff of whiteness escaping her mouth. "First of all, you need to know that I met Ian ten years ago. We'd been together for over four years by the time you came along."

Brandy said nothing for a full minute. Closing her eyes, she tucked Kyle tighter against her. My, but Julie *was* the blunt type, wasn't she? "Does this nightmare ever end? You mean *I* was the mistress at first?"

Julie snickered. "You betcha, baby. And I hated you with a passion. But I knew you didn't know about me, so how could I hold it against you?"

Brandy's head fell back against the top rung of the swing. Staring into the blue of the sky, hearing the songs of the blue jays and cardinals as they braved the cold to root through the bird feeder that swung nearby in a bare maple tree—and sitting shoulder-to-shoulder with her deceased husband's mistress—she snorted, "So why didn't *you* marry him then? If you would've, I wouldn't be going through this nightmare."

"Marriage is the ultimate skin-me-alive-and-lay-my-soul-bare risk. I was happy being single. But I loved Ian. And to his credit, he spent the entire first four years of our relationship trying to convince me to marry him. Then he met you..."

Brandy studied her enemy, noting the strong profile of a woman that, despite the raw-boned sickly look of her now, was without a doubt, a beautiful woman. It was clear that Kyle had inherited the Saxon likeness...except for the eyes.

"Am I supposed to apologize for something I didn't even have a clue about?" she asked, more gently than she'd intended.

Julie turned her head and stared bravely into Brandy's defiant eyes. "No. I'm apologizing to you for my allowing it to happen."

Her eyes were only a shade darker than Dante's, but they had that same exotic shape to them. Brandy was surprised to see them fill with tears. "Oh, please, Julie. Don't cry." Brandy shifted Kyle, his breathing now steady as he napped against her breast, and placed a mittened hand over Julie's leg.

"Tough Julie? Cry?" she asked bitterly, the tears falling like sleet over her chiseled cheekbones. "Rarely have I cried," she admitted, wiping the moisture away with her mitten.

"But crying is healthy," Brandy insisted, returning her hand to pat Kyle's back. "God knows I've produced gallons."

Julie swung her gaze out to the land that would be her son's. It was beautiful, the way the sun glimmered off the surface of the snow, like diamonds scattered over the rolling hills. He would run and play there some day, climb those trees with their stiff black limbs scratching the sky, wade in the spring-fed creek. She could see him there, his dark hair ruffling in the spring breeze as he giggled with glee at a squirrel scurrying up an oak tree, could envision him walking hand-in-hand with them across this land.

When Julie's eyes glazed, Brandy felt an urgency to have all her questions quickly answered. Blurting out one that was foremost in her mind, she asked, "Why did you wait almost a year to come here and tell me all this?"

She sighed. "Because I thought I had a chance at survival. It wasn't until recently that I faced the fact that I'm slowly keeling over."

"But what does your living or dying have to do with whether you claim Kyle's inheritance or not?"

"I'm a stubborn, proud woman. I would have gone on and raised my son alone, provided him with his own inheritance…if I weren't dying. You would never have known I existed."

"But—but, I don't understand." When Julie remained silent, Brandy concluded that it took a woman to die for she herself to finally know her own husband. How ironic.

"Dante's a good man, you know," Julie finally steered the conversation her way and challenged Brandy, for there was little time left to seal her plans.

Brandy scanned the very scenery that Julie eyed, loving the way Kyle's soft hair brushed her jaw. "Maybe a bit deceitful."

"No, he's not," she considered thoughtfully. "It's true, I wanted to tell you as soon as we arrived here, he didn't—he truly loathed the idea of hurting you. But Dante has always ruled with caution. He learned that on the streets as a child."

Again, it pained Brandy to think of them, of any child, enduring such a terrible childhood. Giving them another push with her boot, she admitted, "I'm sorry you two had to go through that. No child should have to live that way."

"Hmm," Julie nodded weakly, thinking of Kyle's future. "Our mother died of cancer when I was five, Dante eight," she flashed their life before Brandy, in a rush now to end it all. "Our father lost it. Left us alone for weeks at a time going on drunken binges. Social Services stepped in. We were placed together, at first, in a nice home outside Chicago."

"Julie, you don't have to relive all this. There's no need to open up old wounds," Brandy assured her, seeing the tears begin anew in Julie's dark eyes.

She coughed heavily. "Wounds like that never heal," she said with a raspy voice.

Yes, Brandy thought sadly, thinking instantly of little Brian's kidnapping. It was true. Some wounds never healed. The wounds that Ian had inflicted on her were already healed, despite the fact that new ones, even now, were being sliced wide open. But there were others that would never heal.

"Well, anyway," Julie went on, "I was abused by that wonderful foster father."

Brandy gasped, her heart aching for the little girl.

"Dante knew, even at the age of almost nine. We ran away, lived on the streets like I told you." Julie smiled lamely. "Dante took such good care of me—for a nine-year-old. After two, maybe three years, I don't know, we were snatched up again by Social Services when Dante was caught stealing a loaf of bread. That's when we were separated."

Brandy sat in total shock, feeling such pity for those innocent children doing their best to survive on the streets. She envisioned a young Dante, his eyes hungry as they locked onto that loaf of bread, his stomach growling painfully. How could she remain pissed at a man who'd been through such turmoil in his life? "Julie…"

Julie punched a hand out of the sleeping bag, holding up a bony palm in protest. "No. I need to tell you this, for Kyle's sake…"

Brandy's brows came together. "For Kyle's sake?"

"Just listen. After we were separated, Dante went on to a good family. Got a good education, learned some manners. Me? It was the luck of the draw. I ended up with another abuser, so I ran away again. Then one day, after years of a pathetic lifestyle of self-destruction, Ian just appeared. He was my savior. With Dante gone from my life, Ian was then the one to get me out of that hell."

Brandy could just see Ian, enamored by the stunning Julie Saxon, seductive, beautiful, unattainable. "And he and Dante met through you," Brandy concluded.

"Exactly. Dante, Mr. Big Shot lawyer by this time, showed up on our doorstep." She shook her head in amazement. "God, how I'd missed him. No one's ever loved me like my big brother. He took so many risks on the streets, just to protect me."

As he now protects me, Julie thought, *cares for me, lovingly sacrifices his own time, bringing me here to die, here where my son will grow up…*

Brandy wasn't sure how much more of this she could take. She was still miffed at Dante, but with every word Julie spoke, she could feel her heart melting.

A long pause came then, and they both inhaled, took in the peace of the countryside, relaxed in acceptance of one another.

"Should we go inside where it's warm now?" Brandy glanced at Julie, her eyes glazed with pure, resigned acceptance.

Julie inhaled the crisp air, filling her lungs, cleansing them, much as she had cleansed her soul for the last twenty minutes. It felt good to have the weight off her shoulders. But there was more…

"Mmm," Julie agreed, nodding dreamily as she watched the eagle soar overhead, it's wings spread lazily on the gentle winter breeze, gliding, searching for a place to call home. "But just one more thing."

Brandy sighed a wavering response, squeezing little Kyle tightly as he began to stir.

"I waited nearly a year to come here," Julie finally addressed the question Brandy had posed some time ago, "because back then, Kyle already had a mother who could care for and support him. I'm here to see that he continues to have one."

Brandy dug her toe into the snow, halting the swing of the glider.

"So now," Julie barreled on in a rush to be done with things, "if you don't agree to become his new mother and adopt him, I'll sell my half of the inn. I already have an eager buyer waiting for me to accept his offer."

CHAPTER 8

❀

She was *furious*!

How could someone force her to adopt a child, for God's sake, against her will? Never mind the fact that she'd become enamored of the little angel-faced imp. It was sheer blackmail! Pacing frantically in the office, she whirled just in time to slam against the wall of Boomer's chest.

"Whoa!" Boomer held up his hands in defense.

"You won't believe it," she began, clenching her fists. "Julie Saxon's forcing me to adopt him. If I don't, I'm faced with a partnership against my will."

"What? Wait just a minute," Boomer perched his massive body onto the corner of her desk. "Rewind, baby. Rewind."

Brandy waved a hand at him, spinning about to retrace her steps. "It's a long story. And I don't have time to go into it. I've got to call my lawyer." Blowing out a breath, she added, "Boomer, I've never been more confused in my life. Ian's really left me in a mess."

"That's nothing new," came a sweet voice from the foyer.

They both turned to see a woman, tall, auburn-haired, slim and elegant, leaning her elbows on the office window overhang, her chin propped on intertwined fingers.

"Natalie!" Brandy screeched, shooting through the office door and out into the foyer to be enfolded in her sister's firm embrace. "How did you get here in all this snow?"

Natalie smiled warmly. "The main highways were cleared—until I got to Platteville. Then I found a shop that rents snowmobiles," her voice rose in delight, her smoky blue eyes twinkling as she studied Brandy at arm's length. "I hitched a ride."

Brandy sighed. "I'm *so* glad you're here."

"So how are you, honey?" Natalie's arms came around her sister protectively. Over her head, she glanced up into eyes like sweet chocolate cream.

"She's going to lose it if we don't get the Saxons out of here soon," Boomer warned, exiting into the foyer and extending a bear-paw-sized hand. "Hi. I'm Boomer Ludwick, Brandy's assistant."

Natalie paused, slowly releasing her sister. There was something quite arresting about the man, all charm, confidence, and striking dark looks, with a faint element of danger underneath. Coolly, she offered her hand to him.

"Pleased to meet you, ah, Boomer, was it?" she asked with a trace of condescension.

He gripped Natalie's hand, noting the slender grace, the slight quiver. The poise with which she presented herself was as thick as bricks. Ms. Cool. That's who she was, he mused. Ms. High and Mighty, too good to be shaking the hand of some former gang member.

"Boomer's been my savior," Brandy offered, her brows drawing together at the sudden tension in the air. "That's more than Ian could ever say."

In the office, a round crystal paperweight trembled, wobbled across the desk, came crashing to the floor. The loud thump was followed by a methodical grinding as it rolled over the wooden planks.

Natalie snatched her hand from Boomer's, startled by the electricity that snapped in the atmosphere, nervously eyeing the glass ball that came to rest near her feet. Rubbing her hand, she replied, "Ian was a no good, sonofa—" she was suddenly thrown against Boomer's thick chest. "What the hell...?"

He steadied her, his breath catching at the sweet scent, the softness of her. "You okay?"

"Natalie?" Brandy blew out a breath and waved a hand, unfazed by the bizarre things that'd been occurring in her house. "Hell, she's always all right. Did I ever tell you, Boomer, that my sister's a doctor?"

Boomer released his hold on the trim arms and propped his elbows on the window ledge behind him. "No. No, you didn't." His instincts were always sharp, street smart. This Natalie chick was as snooty as they came.

"Yep," Brandy beamed, momentarily forgetting the dilemma she was in. "She's a psychiatrist." Then with the briefest pause, her brows went down. Hmm, she could use a shrink about right now, herself.

Boomer swept the length of the doctor, all supple and willowy, as she lifted her straight nose-ever-so-slightly into the air. He noted the full lips, heart-shaped...made for...devouring. Her eyes were an arresting sultry gray, almond-shaped below finely arched dark brows. Her hair was the shade of cinnamon, and she wore it in a knot at the back of her head. Wrapped in a snug ski suit that did little to hide her lithe frame, a whole head taller than Brandy, she was a snobbish package of pure danger.

An involuntary thrill went through Natalie as she glimpsed the corded tawny forearms, the edge of a tattoo peeking out of the rolled up dress shirt sleeves. From the dark, piercing eyes to the sensual lips drawn now in derision, Natalie was completely flustered. Despite the silk tie and impeccable neatness of his attire, he exuded a hidden esoteric aura that both thrilled and frightened her.

For the first time, she seriously questioned the wisdom of coming here.

"Boomer?" Brandy sliced through the unease in the lobby.

Boomer swung his cocoa eyes to her. "What?"

"Did you hear me?"

"Oh, yes, I heard you," he returned his gaze, with little effort, to the cool cucumber. "She's a goddamned shrink."

"Boomer!"

"That's quite all right, Brandy," Natalie folded her arms against her chest. "Some people feel the need to put others down just to make themselves feel bigger...even when they've already got a head big enough to fill the state of Wisconsin."

"Natalie...I—okay," Brandy combed a hand through her loose tendrils. "I don't know what happened here, but let's just start over. Come on, I'll show you around, then settle you in one of the suites."

Boomer's eyes narrowed tightly as the woman eagerly bent to retrieve one of her suitcases. She spun on her booted heel and trailed Brandy up the stairs, her eyes slicing downward to singe him with a look of pure loathing.

"It's a lovely place, Brandy," Natalie scanned the suite, situated toward the rear of the inn above the kitchen. It was furnished with a rich mahogany four-poster queen-sized bed, matching dressing table and armoire, while a hot tub steamed in the chill of the day off the covered balcony. Beyond the secluded porch, she could see the gently rolling hills rippling like soft cotton, until they met the blue of the horizon, broken only by the black branches of the many barren trees. A sparkling creek, edged with slick snow, fed a crescent-shaped lake just beyond the copse, glazed with a thick layer of ice. It was, Natalie thought with some reluctance, a place that would inspire anyone to settle down and live a serene country life.

"Thanks. I thought you might like access to the hot tub until I have to use the room for guests—if anymore ever show up," she muttered half to herself. "I'm doing my best to keep the inn as welcoming as possible. I want my guests to return, do the word-of-mouth thing."

Sliding out of her ski suit, Natalie flopped back on the quilted bed, stretching her svelte form. She exuded refinement, even dressed in jeans and a blue cashmere sweater. "Honey, they will," she assured her sister, yawning. "They will."

"You're tired," Brandy straightened the vines of a potted plant perched on an oak shelf near the window. "I'll let you get some rest."

"Mmm," Natalie fluffed a pillow and stuffed it under her cheek. "I may take you up on that. But I do need to fetch the rest of my luggage downstairs."

"Oh, I'll have Boomer bring it up later," Brandy suggested, crossing to the door.

"No!" Natalie sat upright, her gray eyes like two large winter clouds in a pale sky.

"Why not?"

Natalie shrugged and fell back onto the pillow. "He just makes me...uncomfortable." Natalie's eyes drooped while she muffled another yawn. "There's just something about him. He's too...intense."

Brandy tucked her tongue in her cheek. "I see. Well, we'll discuss it when you get up."

"Brandy?"

"Yes?"

"What was all that talk of adoption and a forced partnership?"

She clamped her jaw in remembrance of what had transpired earlier that day, then turned the knob and stepped into the hallway. Poking her head back in, she replied, "Believe me, I'll fill you in. Just get some rest now."

Natalie couldn't argue with that. She'd been up since four that morning, put in a half day at the clinic, then spent the rest of the afternoon traveling. Rest, she sighed, pulling the blankets over her. She would take a quick power nap, then help Brandy untangle the newest complication in her life.

Boomer, she thought with disgust. What an odd, yet fitting name. As she drifted off to sleep, she imagined those dark eyes and hands as they overtook her. It had quite a booming effect.

"I have some...news, Brandy," Natalie sat at the table in the kitchen nook, plucked a piece of leftover turkey and popped it into her mouth.

Brandy paused, then snapped the walk-in cooler door shut. "That sounds pretty ominous."

Natalie swallowed, then lifted a cup of tea to her lips. Over the rim, she mumbled, "Maxine's coming."

Brandy pulled out a chair from the small kitchen table tucked into the bay window. Distracted, sitting across from her sister, she poured herself a cup of the warm brew. "What did you say?"

Oh, how Natalie dreaded this. "I said, Maxine—you remember our mother?—is coming for a visit. Here. To the inn."

"*What?!*" Brandy dropped her cup onto the saucer and slapped both hands on the surface of the table. "Did you say she was coming? *Here?*"

Natalie nodded, lowering her eyes to contemplate which dessert she would sample—and simultaneously avoiding the steam in her sister's eyes. "Yes."

"Yes?" Brandy slid the pumpkin pie out of Natalie's reach. "Yes is all you can say? How, Natalie? How did she find out where I'm at?"

Natalie wrenched the pie plate from Brandy's grasp and placed a slice on a dessert dish. "I didn't tell her, I swear."

"Then how does she know where I am?" Brandy demanded, rising when the oven timer buzzed.

"She called the hotel where you last worked in New York. She got a hold of some talkative little PBX operator who mentioned that you moved to Mystic, Wisconsin, to open your own bed and breakfast."

"Great. Just great." Brandy's world suddenly became more gray, more complex than before. Pulling the steaming turkey casserole from the oven, she slammed the door shut. "When is she coming?"

Natalie cleared her throat and plopped a heaping of whipped cream on her pie. "Christmas."

Oh, how she could just feel her blood pressure rising by the second! Max sticking her nose in where it didn't belong, Max berating her for every little detail, Max blaming her for Brian's disappearance and their father's suicide. *Just* what she needed to top off the situation with Julie and Dante.

"Wonderful," Brandy snarled. "My life's an open book for everybody."

"And I'm craving a good book to read..." Dante's deep voice flowed across the room.

Both she and Natalie turned at the alluring sound, their eyes jointly coming to rest on him as he stood just inside the kitchen clad in a blue Chicago Bears sweatshirt.

Brandy flushed as the underlying meaning of his words brought a sly smile from Natalie. "Casserole's ready. I was going to prepare a tray for the three of you."

Dante dismissed her words, suddenly interested in the sleek, natural beauty of the woman who bore a striking resemblance to Brandy. But where Brandy was all golden and dazzling, this woman was a darker version, more refined and aloof. Even from across the room, he noted the cloudy gray of her eyes, eyes that seemed to scan him like a computer would for viruses.

"Who's your guest?" he asked as he sauntered forward, riveting his eyes back to Brandy, taking in the jeans and tight green knit shirt she wore like a second skin.

With a glare of annoyance, Brandy grudgingly made the introductions. "My sister, Dr. Natalie Hart. Natalie, this is Dante Saxon, Ian's former attorney and friend."

Ah, a connection to the slime bag, Natalie thought before rising to extend her hand. When the large, warm hand gripped hers firmly, she surmised that Ian had lucked out with this man. A handshake spoke volumes.

Smiling coolly, she lowered herself to her seat and replied, "So very pleased to meet you, Mr. Saxon."

"Dante. Please. I wasn't aware Brandy had family nearby."

"Oh, yes." Natalie returned to her pie, slipping a small forkful into her mouth. "My mother and I live near Chicago in the suburbs."

Strange. He hadn't seen anyone near her at the funeral, comforting her as family would. "Well, welcome. I'll just fill up our tray and take my sister and nephew up some dinner. Was nice meeting you."

"You too, Mr. Saxon—um, Dante," she revised as he raised a brow at her. She watched with interest as Brandy's gaze swept him, then locked tightly with his own smoldering one. Quietly, they merged and stood side-by-side loading a large room service tray with casserole, turkey sandwiches, salad.

He strolled from the room with a nod to her, holding the tray carefully before him, and Natalie noted the tall, dark bulk of him, all raw and masculine, as graceful and handsome as an Indian warrior. Clucking her tongue, she followed his departure until he was out of range.

"Don't strain your neck, Natalie," Brandy warned, returning to her seat.

She swung her eyes back to her sister, a mischievous twinkle in the depths of them. "He's a very alarming man. I detect something there between you two…"

Alarming was only half of it, Brandy seethed inside. "You know I don't like talking about my personal life."

"You're sleeping with him." It wasn't an accusation. It was an observation.

"Natalie!"

Grinning slyly, she broke off the crust of her pie and pointed it at Brandy before gnawing on it. "I'm right, aren't I?"

"You know," Brandy hissed. "You're more like Maxine than I realized."

"I'm right," Natalie concluded, deflecting the insult as any good therapist would.

"He's the brother of Ian's former mistress, who happens to be upstairs with her toddler son, and dying of cancer minute-by-minute under my very roof."

She blinked, shifted in her seat. "You're kidding," she replied gently, slowly lowering her hand to cover Brandy's. She hadn't an inkling until now that the situation ran that deep and bizarre for her sister. And her heart instantly ached for her. *Ian, you bastard*, she thought.

"No. And they've come to inform me that Ian left half the inn to *her.*" Brandy's eyes wandered around the room that'd become her pride and pleasure. Would she lose it all? she wondered painfully. "She's demanding that I adopt her son before she dies—which isn't far off—or she'll sell her half of this place to a stranger."

Natalie's eyes widened considerably. "Oh, honey. You must feel so trapped, so betrayed. How can she do such a thing to you?"

She shook her head passionately. "If Ian were here right now," Brandy clenched her jaw, "I'd strangle him. I'd be much more deadly than that car accident ever was. No lie."

You and me both, Natalie thought, then replied, "That's good," she nodded her approval. "You have to let it out, express your anger."

Brandy simply rolled her eyes. Boomer was right. Her sister *was* a damn shrink.

"You're feeling betrayed by Ian, a natural response," she said soothingly, the expert at dealing with emotions, slyly manipulating them from her subject.

But even Natalie was human. The suspense was killing her. "What do you suppose you'll do?"

Face in her hands, Brandy groaned, "Adopt him."

"*What?!*" Natalie shrieked.

Combing her hands through her hair, Brandy faintly snarled, "You heard me. I said I'm going to try and adopt him."

"You're going to adopt Ian's illegitimate son?" Natalie's eyes were broad pools of smoke, her jaw a wide open cave. When she got no response from her sister, she pleaded, "Brandy, honey, you've got to rethink this. Look at all the responsibilities you already have with the inn. Besides, a woman just doesn't up and adopt her dead husband's illegitimate son, the product of his affair with his mistress. How are you going to have time to raise a child? And why in the world doesn't *that* man just adopt his own nephew?" Natalie rambled on, gesturing toward the arched doorway where Dante had exited moments ago.

She hadn't thought of that, hadn't wanted to. She'd only been remembering the baby scent, the soft bundle that had twice snuggled lovingly against her breast, the little mischievous baby with Ian's eyes and Dante's coloring—and the fact that she didn't want to lose her inn. It hadn't taken her long to get over the shock of Julie's coercion, to realize that she *would* adopt Ian's son, but not just to keep the inn from falling into the hands of a stranger.

Kyle had already stolen her heart.

And Dante had broken it, she thought sourly, denying that the urge for revenge weighed partially in her decision.

Soon Kyle would be motherless, and even she couldn't allow Ian's child to be raised without a mother to love and guide him, despite the fact that the child was the obvious evidence of an unfaithful husband.

"Dante is a busy lawyer," she rationalized. "He's not going to have time to take care of a toddler, nor is he going to want to."

"You're wrong there," Dante was back, filling the archway menacingly. He strolled to the refrigerator and snatched up two bottles of Pepsi.

Brandy's eyes narrowed. "What do you mean, I'm wrong? There's no way you'll have time for him."

Dante whirled on her, the bottles clinking together in his hand. "And you think you're going to have more time than me? You're running an inn, for Christ's sake. Besides," he came forward and set the bottles aside to plant his palms on the table before her, spearing her with the sharp arrow of his golden eyes, "he's my nephew by *blood*. I've been helping to raise him since he was a newborn baby."

"Because *you* knew he existed!" Brandy spat, shooting so quickly to her feet that her chair crashed to the hardwood floor.

Natalie only blinked, recognizing the constructive release of emotions. This was an interesting scenario, and she saw no need to interfere. Crossing her arms over her chest, she watched the drama unfold, her gaze bouncing back and forth as if she watched an intense tennis match.

"Yes, I'll give you that," Dante conceded as he rose to his full menacing height. "But that doesn't change the fact that he's more attached to me than he ever was to Ian. I'm like a father to him, and you're not going to take his father figure from him."

"He needs a mother," Brandy used the only bit of defense she could think of. "I can give him all he needs right here. He'll be home with me, not in a daycare."

"He's used to it. He likes preschool."

"You already take him to daycare?" she screeched her question.

"Of course. I can't leave him with Julie as sick as she is. And I have to work."

Brandy snorted, slapping her hands to her hips. "He's not even two. Preschool is for older children, not toddlers. It's nothing more than baby sitting, and you know it. He'll get so much more attention here with me than at a daycare with dozens of other kids running around begging to be loved."

"As I recall, your inn can get pretty busy too." Dante snatched up the soft drinks and jabbed a bottle at her. "Now back off, Brandy. You're not getting him. He's my flesh and blood, not yours!" He was trembling inside, sick at the thought of losing Kyle. Damn you, Julie, and your idiotic plans, his mind shouted. And damn you, Ian, for putting us both in this goddamn mess.

"Go ahead, use hurtful facts to bring me down. But hear this, Dante," Brandy warned, leaning dangerously close to the Pepsi weapon he wielded. "I'm getting a lawyer. And given Ian's infidelity, I'll have a big advantage in winning custody of his son—*my* stepson."

He ignored her point and studied the determined green sparkle in her eyes, eyes that less than twelve hours ago, had smoldered with passion for him. Now, they burned with a near-hatred that made him long to kiss her, to soothe the fear that was the basis for her rancor.

Shifting, again setting the drinks aside, he gripped her upper arms and stared deep into her eyes. "Look, Brandy," he blew out a breath, inhaled deeply. "Now's not the time to discuss custody battles. Julie's close, so close that *I'll* be planning a funeral by Christmas. For Julie's sake," he gently shook her, "let's lay this to rest…for now."

She studied the dark rings around the gold of his eyes, remembering how they could smolder to a shimmering brown. "Yes, for Ian's mistress' sake, I'll keep my talk of lawyers and adoption and custody all to myself."

Watching with fascination as the muscle along his strong jaw quivered, lips thinning, Brandy felt a chill wrack her. Those very lips had been buried in the most intimate of places not so long ago. A mistake as far as she was concerned, especially given the fact that, as Ian's lawyer, he'd known all along that Ian had left half the inn to Julie. He'd known, and still taken carnal advantage of her…

"For now…" Dante growled, releasing her as if she'd stung him. Plucking up the Pepsis once more, he stalked from the room, gripping the bottles so tightly, his knuckles whitened.

Brandy watched in tense stillness as he disappeared from sight.

"Now that's what I call productive communication," Natalie furtively watched the empty doorway as she spoke to break the deafening silence.

Brandy's stare shot to her sister like radar locking onto its target. "Go to hell, Natalie," and she exited the room leaving Natalie feeling less than professionally adequate.

CHAPTER 9

❀

As Monday neared, Julie's health began to decline rapidly. Dante sat vigil at her bedside holding her hand, while Kyle toddled around the room, opening drawers, unloading suitcases, fishing in the toilet.

The soft rap barely registered in Dante's tired mind. He was completely exhausted, rising in the middle of the night to tend both Julie and Kyle.

"Come in," he said gruffly.

Natalie peeped around the door, her dark red hair twisted at the back of her head. "Brought you some dinner," she smiled softly, entering the room with a tray.

"Num-num!" Kyle squealed, barreling across the room to throw his arms around Natalie's legs. "Mmm!"

She patted the dark head, holding the tray expertly with one arm, recalling the feel of Brian's soft, baby-fine hair. "You're a hungry little monster, huh?"

"I mon-ter," Kyle agreed, rocking his body against her legs as he tipped his head back with a ravenous glaze in his eyes. "I hun-gee!"

Natalie giggled softly, taking his tiny hand in hers. She crossed to the small dining table set near the sliding glass door, noting the laptop attached to a modem, the law books spread out on the table and nearby floor, the stacks and piles of paperwork. The man was burning his emotional and psychological candles at both ends, she deduced silently feeling a large measure of compassion for him. Placing the tray upon the table, she lifted Kyle into the cushioned seat and prepared his plate.

"Now you be a good boy and don't make a mess," she said, ruffling Kyle's hair.

Dante watched the display, accepting the fact that Kyle seemed to be able to adapt to anyone, anywhere…just like his dad. "Thanks. He's been a terror the last hour or so."

"You really should eat too. Go on over there with him," Natalie ordered. "I'll sit with her for awhile," she assured him, her eyes caressing his two-day stubble, the gray smudges under tired eyes, the unkempt hair and clothing.

Dante hesitated momentarily, then gently lowered Julie's bony hand to the bed. "She's been sleeping all day, even through Kyle's fits. Except for waking to vomit." He wearily crossed the room to sit with Kyle.

Natalie took the seat Dante had vacated and began sponging Julie's perspiring brow. The woman was like an ashen skeleton, and she objectively assessed that Ian's kept mistress would soon be passing on into another life.

"Did she have treatments, chemo, radiation?" Natalie asked, glancing over to see both child and uncle chowing down on beef stew and biscuits.

"Yes," Dante said between mouthfuls. "All of the above. It was just detected too late. She even had a mastectomy."

Natalie had already surmised as much. "I'm so sorry. It must be very hard for you to see her like this." It was apparent he loved his sister deeply. There weren't too many men who would put their lives on hold to cater to a sister's last rites.

He nodded as he sopped up the stew with a torn biscuit, giving Kyle the other half. "It's ironic that cancer is going to kill her, when she'd triumphed over some tough odds as a kid."

"Life isn't always fair. Brandy can attest to that," Natalie declared, taking Julie's hand in her own.

"Brandy's a puzzling woman, for sure."

"Did she ever tell you about our little Brian?"

Dante pushed his bowl away and drained his glass of milk. Lifting Kyle's cup, he held the rim carefully to the smeared lips. Kyle gulped the milk as heavily as his uncle had. "No. Who's Brian?"

"Our little brother. He was kidnapped when he was a bit older than Kyle. Brandy had been baby sitting. Maxine's always blamed her—but our mother's another story. Brandy was only thirteen at the time. Shortly afterward, our father committed suicide. Maxine's always blamed Brandy. Supposedly, Dad killed himself due to the stress of the kidnapping. She's never forgiven Brandy, and Brandy's always fled from the pain, the blame, the shunning."

Her words filled in the missing puzzle pieces of the complex Brandy. He analyzed Kyle, trying to imagine how devastating it would be to have him snatched, to never know where he was, if he were okay, alive. And worse, to feel that you were to blame. The baggage she must be carrying with her…

"I'm…sorry. Brandy never mentioned it."

"No," Natalie surmised, watching closely as Julie began to stir. "Brandy has always guarded herself very carefully. She can't take much more pain."

Dante caught the subtle leading-of-the-witness ploy. "Boomer says you're a shrink."

And Boomer should just mind his own damn business. "No, I'm a psychiatrist."

"You play the part well," Dante said smoothly. "Very soothing and therapeutic. Calm. Cool."

Julie moaned, as if sensing the rising tension in the air. Kyle leaped from his chair and squealed, "Ma-ma!" as he tottered across the room toward the bed.

"Kyle!" Dante's roaring voice echoed in the room.

Startled, Kyle fell to the floor and plopped onto his diapered behind.

"Come here," Dante ordered. "Let me wipe you off before you go smearing all that goop all over Mom."

Kyle obeyed, presenting his hands and face to his uncle. When he was released from the strong hold, he stumbled to the bed and climbed in next to Julie.

"Oh…hi…punky," Julie's eyes fluttered open as she sensed her son's presence.

Natalie cringed at the sunken dark eyes, the cracked lips, the labored respirations. Yes, she was definitely at death's door. "How are you feeling, honey?" Natalie asked, bringing a cup of water to Julie's mouth.

Julie eyed the svelte woman warily, but obediently took a sip of the cool water. "Who…are you?"

"I'm Natalie Hart, Brandy's sister. Helping out for a bit."

Ah. Another pawn in the game to help secure Kyle's future, Julie mused. "How…kind…of you," Julie croaked, coughing coarsely.

"Dante," Natalie quickly formed a plan. He and Brandy needed time together. "Why don't you run along with Kyle. You could both use a few minutes to stretch your legs. You've been cooped up in here forever."

Dante eyed the woman suspiciously, but the thought of getting out into the fresh air had him ignoring his instincts. "You're sure you don't mind sitting with her?"

Julie lifted a trembling, stick-thin arm. "Go…Dante. You hover…too much."

Plucking Kyle from the middle of the bed, he growled, "Come on, little guy. Let's go hunt up some dessert."

Kyle's chubby face cracked a wide grin. "Yummy, yummy!" he readily agreed, urging his uncle with a few anxious pats on the back.

Watching her brother and son go, Julie said hoarsely, "Ms. Hart? Natalie?"

"Yes?"

"I need your help."

It was her job, her calling, to help those in turmoil. The declaration didn't surprise her. "I agree."

"I love my son...more than life itself," her bulging brown eyes slowly turned upon Natalie.

Natalie reached for the frail hand. "He's a beautiful child."

"I'd hoped to have more...energy when I arrived here," she whispered, her eyes sparkling with diamond-like tears. "And time is my enemy. I wanted to be assured...that he'd have both a mother—" the wracking cough brought her upright in bed, "and father."

Natalie reached for a tissue and held it over Julie's mouth where red-tinged phlegm had begun to ooze. Slowly, she lowered Julie back to the pillow. "That's a rather selfless plan."

"My brother would strongly disagree with you."

"Dante will, in the end, do what's best for Kyle."

"If at all possible," Julie gasped for each breath, "I want him to have..." she raised a hand to weakly grip Natalie's arm, her eyes beseeching the other woman, "both parents—together, here in this beautiful home."

"So you've devised a plan to coerce my sister into being his mother," Natalie's voice was soothing, matter-of-fact. "And you've always known that Dante would never abandon him as the father figure."

Julie smiled feebly, triumphantly. "They're perfect for each other. Together, they'd be ideal parents for him."

At Natalie's silence, she continued. "Ian's been visiting me. He's enraged."

"Really?" her hand reached again for the wet rag and tightened on it. She twisted the cool water from it before placing it back on Julie's forehead. Yes, Ian would make the perfect asshole ghost, Natalie snickered silently.

Julie nodded, amused with herself for believing such a crock. Ghosts, haunted houses, spirits able to permeate reality. There was a time she'd have been the worst cynic of all. Yet he'd been here standing at the side of her bed, as clear as Natalie now was. "He seems to think Brandy…should become an old maid."

Natalie chuckled melodically. "Ian was always quite chauvinistic."

"Yes. But he'll see it my way…for Kyle's sake."

"I've never met you before today, Julie," she sponged the perspiring brow and searched the pained dark depths of eyes that were slowly dying. Ghosts weren't her expertise. Feelings and emotions were. "But I think, whether you care to admit it or not, you're a selfless woman full of love and kindness."

Pausing for a moment at the shocked expression on the grayish face, Natalie added with a sly grin, "Dante and Brandy," she considered, cocking her head. "They *are* perfect for each other, aren't they?"

Except for the drop-in guests who'd just arrived, a young couple sitting at a cozy corner table staring lovingly at one another over a dancing candle, the dining room was empty. They held hands and whispered soft words, now and then giggling, kissing, caressing one another.

Dante shifted uncomfortably in his stance, taking a large plate and piling it with fruit, walnut-covered brownies, and a variety of cookies from a sample tray. He had to hand it to Brandy. She was an excellent cook, just as good as her chef who'd been out the entire week. Her warm hospitality was to be commended as well, but he'd be damned, he thought, clutching Kyle tightly against his side, if he'd allow Kyle to live here, to be apart from him, no matter how accommodating she was.

Kyle should be with familiar family. *Kyle should be with me*, the words echoed in his head.

They went to the lounge, and Dante stood Kyle on a chair in front of a video game where he watched the neon lights and listened to the clinks and clanks with fascination, sure he was controlling the game as it ran its demo over and over. Planting himself nearby at the computer, Dante signed onto the Internet, knowing he could get more work done if Kyle were occupied here rather than upstairs disturbing Julie.

As he waited for it to load, his thoughts once again went to *her*. Sensual, provocative, seductively perilous with all those curves and soft spots. She'd come alive in his arms, casting a spell that'd become somehow more irreversible with the adoption threats she now held over his head. Over the last three days, he'd found himself painfully and ashamedly erect in broad daylight, remembering her scent, her husky little moans and murmurs, the softness of her skin.

But that was all he would have, he decided with determination as he studied Kyle, watching him pound buttons and squeal with delight. The memory of it.

He emailed his partner at the firm, briefly explaining the situation, and asking him to prepare a custody case. Because, he thought darkly, looking over again at the delighted, screeching nephew that he'd come to regard as a son. No one, not even a woman with the irresistible charms of a dangerous witch, was going to take Kyle from him.

"Brandy..." Julie had called for her the next day, her breathing becoming more ragged. "Please promise me...that you'll...adopt Kyle. Please."

Dante had left them alone at Julie's insistence, and Brandy was able to speak freely. "It didn't take me long to think it over, Julie. I'll try. I promise. He's Ian's son, and therefore, I'll make him my son."

Julie had already informed her that selling her half of the inn had been nothing but a threat. There was no potential buyer, no one to force a partnership upon her. But that no longer mattered to Brandy. Either way, she'd already decided she would adopt him.

Julie smiled weakly. "Thank...you," her raspy voice was a mere whisper in the dim room. She pictured Dante and Brandy together as a family with her son, and her smile broadened.

Panting between coughs, Julie said, "You're a...good person, Brandy. I'm so sorry...that Ian and I...betrayed you."

"No, no, Julie," Brandy felt her eyes tearing, a bond forming with this remarkable woman, someone who, if things had been different, she could have been close friends with. "Just like you told me, you were with him first. Ian is the one to blame, not you," she declared, noting with defiance the sudden whipping of the drapes over the closed patio door.

"He still...loved you, Brandy," Julie said with some effort, both physically and emotionally.

And a soft wispy caress, as if to underscore Julie's words, ran up Brandy's spine.

She placed a hand on her brow and petted the smoothness of it, driving to the back of her mind the memory of the odd force that had nearly kept her from entering Julie's room and approaching her beside. "And he loved you too, Julie, or he wouldn't have gone to such lengths to see that you and Kyle were provided for."

Julie snorted, then a coarse cough erupted. Brandy released Julie's hand and placed a tissue in it. Julie covered her mouth, coughing up bloody mucous. With the cancer invading her lungs and her immune system depleted from the chemotherapy, she'd inherited Kyle's flu.

"But what would...he have done...if both he and I had lived?" Julie asked sardonically. "Move Kyle...and I...in here...with you?"

Brandy saw the humor in it, and chuckled, "Knowing Ian, yes. He would've at least tried."

She stiffly turned on her side to face Brandy, her face washed purple. Ian was there behind Brandy, beckoning to her. "Could you...get Dante now?"

Brandy shot to her feet, ignoring the odor of sickness and pain. "Are—are you okay?" she felt her heart surge swiftly up into her head and knew a pounding headache to rival all.

"No," she gasped, her eyes bulging, suddenly taking on that far-away look of death. "Please…"

"Yes, I'll get him." Pausing, she bent to place a kiss on Julie's sallow cheek.

Julie smiled endearingly before her eyes began to roll back in her head.

Clutching at her gut, Brandy raced from the room, her heart thudding painfully fast. It was time. She could feel it.

"*Dante!*" she shouted from the top of the stairs, her voice echoing throughout the inn. "*Dante!*"

He zoomed from the recreation room. "What!" he barked up at her, Kyle perched on his hip.

"What is it, Brandy, honey?" Natalie asked, alarmed as she raced from the kitchen.

"It's Julie," she panicked, her eyes returning impatiently to Dante. "Dante, she wants you."

Natalie knew the voice of impending death. It was Julie's time. She'd seen that coming yesterday. Unfastening her apron, she tossed it on the stairs as she followed Dante up to their suite.

When he reached her, her breathing was much more ragged than it'd been when he'd left her moments ago. Julie reached out a cold hand to him. "Dante…Kyle…"

Brandy and Natalie watched from the door, dreading, waiting for what was inevitable. Clamping her teeth together, Brandy struggled to withhold the tears.

"I'm here, Jules. Kyle's here too. Give Mom kisses, Kyle," he said gently, sitting Kyle on the bed in the curve of Julie's gaunt form.

Kyle bent and kissed her pasty cheek. Placing a tiny hand on her jaw, he put his face inches from hers and said softly, "Ma-ma sick?"

"Yes...punkin. Ma-ma's sick," Julie cracked a smile, gasping with each inspiration.

Kyle kissed her on the mouth. "Wuv you Ma-ma," he murmured in a tiny voice.

At the door, Brandy allowed the tears to spill. Natalie looked on serenely, the doctor accepting of death.

"Oh, Kyle...honey," Julie began to cry, pulling him against her flat, bony chest. "Ma-ma loves you, too."

Kyle laid his dark head on her chest and relaxed, squeezing his eyes tightly shut...as if he knew.

"You be a good boy...for Ma-ma...you hear?" she petted his hair, his back, clutching him to her with all the strength she could muster.

"Julie," Dante warned tenderly. "You're going to sap your energy."

She coughed again, spitting up a large pool of bloody secretions. Panting, she looked to her brother. "Dante...I love you. You were the only other...person to...truly care...for me."

"Julie—"

"Shhh," Julie put a shaky finger to her lips. "Listen. Just promise me...you'll do what's...best for him. What we talked about..."

"You know I will, Julie," Dante fell to his knees at the bedside and buried his head on the pillow next to his sister, his arm over her and Kyle. "Julie, please, just rest now. *Please.*"

"Only you know..." she choked, fighting for one more breath, "what I truly...want for him."

"Julie," Dante fought to suppress the emotions. This wasn't happening. *It wasn't!* "Just be quiet and relax. You've got to conserve your energy...Julie?"

She took one last breath, and her eyes opened wide. "Ian?" she gasped as a contented expression washed over her gray face; her arms rose above her, reaching. Then, like a jolt, her body went limp, cold, and her arms fell back around her beloved son.

"Julie?" Dante shook her as Kyle clung to his mother. "*Julie!*"

A hand came to his shoulder. "Dante," Natalie said calmly, gently. "She's gone." Reaching down, she passed a hand over Julie's face and closed the open lids.

"No. *No!*" Dante wailed, pulling Julie's feeble body into his arms, Kyle between them.

Kyle began to whine then, "Ma-ma, Ma-ma!" and Natalie took him carefully from between the man and the corpse.

Brandy watched in utter shock. Never before had she seen a person die before her very eyes, nor a man display such raw emotion. It touched her heart, wrenching it from her chest. She came to him, pulling him to her, his face buried in her abdomen. "Dante," she coaxed softly, fighting tears of her own as one of his hands still held steadfast to his sister. "It's okay. She's in heaven now. She's with Ian. She can finally rest in peace."

Dante gave no indication of having heard her words and reached over to run his hand across Julie's bald head. Slowly, he moved from Brandy and kissed Julie's smooth brow. Brandy pulled him to her once again. This time, he turned, accepting the solace of the woman. There, holding him firmly against her midriff, he on his knees, they cried for the dead woman who'd left them in a terrible plight. Brandy assuaged him in much the same way he'd provided her with comfort at Ian's wake.

He sobbed, clutching her, burying his face in her blouse, and she dropped to her knees, rocking him, soothing the pain. He'd spent his entire life trying to protect Julie, but cancer had finally won out. He'd been no match against the silent killer.

His sister was dead!

With each tear he spent, Brandy felt her soul reaching out to him, entwining with his, and she tried weakly to prevent it, remembering that they were at odds with each other, that she had no business becoming more involved with this man—her new lawyer had already advised her to stay clear of him. And here she was experiencing with him, the very personal, moving death of a loved one.

"Dante," she prompted him gently, lifting his face to hers. His eyes were shimmering gold pools, and the suffering he'd carried with him for decades, was mirrored there as brightly as the hue of them.

Dante looked into her kind green eyes and saw a compassion that touched his spirit. "She's gone," he rasped. "What…what am I going to do now?"

Brandy enfolded him in her arms again, recalling the anguish she'd felt at Ian's passing, never wishing that kind of pain on anyone. "I'm here," she breathed, ignoring the words of her lawyer as they echoed in her head. "I'll help you get through it."

They buried her several days later in a small ancient cemetery just beyond the lake. They'd hired a landscaper with a dozer that was willing to travel the tiny, snow-bound lane that led to the burial ground. Like a godsend, the weather had offered reprieve, and the sun had shone like a golden ball of life upon the pure whiteness of the land, down upon the pale pink casket that had been perched over the deep hole. In the stiff darkness of earth, they'd prepared her a resting place that nestled into the land where she'd chosen to die, where she'd hoped her son would be raised.

Dante stood there now, a week later, gripping Kyle's hand, both of them bundled against the chill of the day. He looked to his nephew, then to the grave with its freshly turned dirt and soggy bouquets that'd been placed there the day of the burial.

Kyle pointed to the mound. "Ma-ma?" he scrunched his face, looking up at the somber expression on his uncle's face.

"Yes, Kyle," Dante squatted down on his haunches, lowering his head to Kyle's eye level. "Mommy got really sick. She's buried here now," he pointed to the simple headstone. "But her soul is in heaven. Ma-ma's an angel now," he smiled softly, watching as Kyle's azure eyes clouded with confusion, rising heavenward. He didn't know if it were true, but it would help Kyle to understand, to accept the absence of his mother.

He saw the movement out of the corner of his eye. When his gaze swung to her, his mind short-circuited. Brandy was dressed in a long wool coat, jeans, and hiking boots. Her hair was loose today, the shimmering wheat-colored tresses blowing gently about her heart-shaped face. Her eyes gleamed with unshed tears, and she stood back hesitantly, holding an arrangement of fresh flowers.

"I went to the florist," she explained, suddenly feeling like an intruder.

Dante rose, detecting the indecision in her manner. "She hated flowers," he joked, his faint grin fading.

"Well, I'll—I'll just give them to you. You can do what you want with them."

She stepped toward him and he was assaulted by her fragrance, the scent of only her mingling with that of the perky blossoms. He took the bundle from her trembling grasp, then handed them to Kyle. "Want to put these on Mommy's grave?"

Kyle's eyes twinkled with mischief. Nodding his dark head vigorously, he reached for the thick bouquet with both hands. Then he went to work, decorating his mommy's new home, scattering the bright blooms haphazardly about the freshly-turned earth.

As Brandy ducked her head and began to turn away, Dante said harshly, "Brandy."

Her head spun quickly around at the tone in his voice, ominous, packed with pain yet to come. "I—I don't want to interfere. I'm sorry I interrupted—"

"You're not imposing," he nearly growled, mentally denying that the beautiful sight of her seemed to infuriate him, even after her self-less support following Julie's passing. And even now, he didn't care to explore why he wanted her to stay and go at the same time. Slim golden beauty and arresting green eyes aside, he suddenly saw her as a threat. Reality was raw. She was going through with the adoption, or at the very least, her lawyer had indicated in his petition that she would be seeking custodial or visitation rights. She wanted to take away the only part of Julie he had left. And he knew he'd never let that happen, in spite of the fact that she'd been a mere pawn in Ian's life.

"I really should get back to the office…"

"Brandy," he came a step closer. "We need to talk."

No. She just didn't want to talk about the custody suit. Not here over Julie's grave, not here in front of the very child it involved.

When she remained silent and fixed her gaze on the child, Dante snarled, "Are you listening?"

She snapped her stare back to him, taking in the firmness of his jaw, the faint five-o'clock shadow, the pain that still burned in his eyes. "Yes, I'm listening. I just don't think this is the time or place to discuss…things."

"I'm leaving," he said as he blew out a breath. "Today."

Her heart stopped. *Leaving?* Why did it surprise her so very much?

She riveted her eyes back to Kyle, happily decorating, climbing about the headstone. He glanced up at her, his eyes like ocean waters, and smiled innocently. Sidestepping Dante, she dropped to her knees over Julie's grave and gathered Kyle into her arms.

"You can't do this to me," she cried, glaring up at Dante, her eyes suddenly resembling grass glimmering with the morning dew. "Please, Dante, don't take him away," she begged in a whisper. "I'll take good care of him while you're away in Chicago."

Kyle dropped the remaining flowers and threw his arms around Brandy, singing, "Mommy!" then promptly planted a wet kiss on her cheek.

Brandy closed her eyes, savoring the softness, the aroma of baby shampoo and grape Kool-Aid. "No, honey, I'm not your mommy. But I want to be. I love you just as much as your real momma," she declared returning the kiss.

Dante's body went stiff with her show of emotion, with Kyle's simple word. Damn her anyway for making this harder on them all. Kyle didn't need to be getting his hopes up, his little mind in confusion. "Brandy, he belongs with me and you know it."

"No!" she rose with Kyle clutched to her breast. "I don't know any such thing. You can't take him and deposit him every day in an uncaring daycare when I'm here, willing to give him as much love as his own mother had."

Kyle kissed her again. "Ma-ma!" he clapped his hands gleefully.

"Kyle, come here!" Dante barked, holding his hands out to the boy. Resentment boiled within him. The child would only call Julie his mother.

Kyle's little black brows furrowed together. He looked in indecision from one somber adult to the other.

"Don't use that tone with him," Brandy warned, twisting her hip so that she could perch Kyle out of Dante's reach.

Dante sighed, then paused in shock.

Only you know what I truly want for him, Julie's voice echoed across the land, through his head—hell, he didn't know where her damn voice had come from. But he'd heard it as clear as he was hearing the birds chirping in the nearby oak tree, and he resisted, refusing to heed the message. What Julie had intended, and what was right for Kyle, were two entirely different things.

And he needed to get back to his life.

"What's wrong?" Brandy startled at the pale tone to his face.

"N-nothing," he snapped. "Now give him back to me."

She stood there, defiantly holding Kyle out of his reach, daring him to shatter her world.

"I have to get back to reality," he nearly roared, reaching around her, snatching Kyle from her gentle hold. "And so should you."

"Dante!" she gasped, grasping frantically for Kyle as he was wrenched from her hold—and her heart.

Kyle whimpered, the tiny scuffle frightening him to tears.

Turning to face her, Dante softened a small measure, ignoring with an effort the loveliness, the gentle beauty of her as she stood like a mother bear prepared to protect her cub. "Look Brandy. I'm sorry, but I have to think of him. This is what's best for him."

"No, Dante," she reached out a trembling hand, gripping the forearm that held Kyle. "Please," she tugged on the arm. "Please don't do this. He's my husband's son, my stepson. He's all I have left…"

So she was still pining for him, even after all Ian had put her through. Even after they'd made love… The thought of it ate away at his gut, making him see her in a pathetic new light. He clamped his jaw, his nostrils flaring as he swept her from head to toe, to head again.

"How pitiful for a woman to still want to hold onto a man who so effortlessly screwed her over," he spat, wrenching her hand from his arm.

Brandy sucked in a ragged breath, and she felt her intended words clog in her throat. He'd shocked her into silence, and he now strode arrogantly from her with the child that she'd grown to love over such a short period. With him he took her only hope at motherhood, her only hope at love.

"Dante," she wept softly. "*Please*. It's not Ian that I love…" she gathered her coat against the sudden gale-force winds that whipped about her, "…it's you."

But he was too far away to hear her declaration, too stubborn to care.

Falling to the mushy soil near Julie's grave, Brandy cried silent tears as yet another child was snatched from beneath her very nose.

CHAPTER 10

"Your only chance is to prove him unfit," Soloman Carver surmised. He was one of two attorneys in Mystic, and the only one she could afford. "He's been with the child since birth. You haven't."

Brandy gripped the phone with both hands. "But he's my husband's *son*—which makes him my stepson."

"Yes," Sol reluctantly agreed. "True. But I can't see a judge on this planet allowing adoption or awarding custody to someone who hadn't even laid eyes on the child until he was one-and-a-half. If that's the argument you want me to play on, well, it's your money. But I don't think you stand a chance."

Brandy suppressed the tears, snatching a tissue from her desktop. "What about the fact that he's practically living in a daycare five days a week? I mean, here I am, self-employed, able to care for him twenty-four hours a day in my own home, and a judge would allow him to be neglected on a daily basis instead?"

"Well," Sol conceded, "you do have that in your favor. And I'll do my best, Mrs. MacKay, to at the very least, get you visitation rights. But I don't want you to get your hopes up. Mr. Saxon is a highly talented and crafty attorney." *And someone I'd love to best*, Sol thought silently.

"Soloman, I don't care if I'm fighting the mob itself. I want custody of that child. It's what the mother wanted, too."

"What do you mean?" Sol saw a glimmer of hope.

"She made me promise on her deathbed that I'd adopt him. It was her dying wish that Kyle have me—her lover's wife—as his mother."

"Really?" Sol's interest was peaked. Reaching for a pen, he jotted a few notes down. "Did you get it on tape or in writing?"

Brandy sighed, seeing too late, the negligence. *Why hadn't she gotten it in writing?* "No."

Soloman was briefly silent, then said, "Well, that would've almost certainly sealed the deal for you, but now, we just need to prove it. Did she mention her wishes to Mr. Saxon, or anyone else?"

"I suspect she might have. I know that the two seemed at odds toward the end, but I really don't know what it was all about."

"Okay," Sol shuffled some papers, anxious to get this ball rolling. "Well, I'll start with what you've given me. If anything else, no matter *how* trivial, pops into your head, call me." *Because it would be such a career accomplishment to best Dante Saxon, shrewd Chicago attorney,* Sol silently foamed at the mouth.

Dante was deeply frustrated. Kyle had kept him up all night, no doubt, missing Julie. As a result, he'd overslept. Ten in the morning. Hell, he usually had a good three hours work in by now.

Unlacing Kyle's shoe for the third time, Dante said firmly, "Hold still Kyle. And quit kicking your shoes off. I've got to get you to Tot Time—like *now.*"

"Why?" Kyle's mouth formed a perplexed O as he challenged Dante with a patient look.

Dante groaned. "Why" had become Kyle's newest word in the weeks since Julie's death. "Because, you booger, I have to go to work. I'm already late."

Kyle crossed his arms over his chest, mimicking his uncle's trademark gesture. "No work, Don-tee."

Retying the shoe, Dante ruffled Kyle's midnight hair. "Son, I have to. Don't you want toys, food, candy?"

Kyle's face bloomed into a delighted grin. "Candy!" he shouted, hopping to his feet to celebrate his uncle's wonderful suggestion.

"No, not now, silly," Dante said scornfully, scooping him up before he zoomed out of reach. "Now, we gotta go."

Taking the elevator from the fifth floor to the parking garage in the basement, Dante once again ignored the little voice of guilt: He'd been the one to purchase Ian's Chicago condo. It was situated nicely in a six block perimeter of everything that he needed, his office, Kyle's daycare, shopping, and restaurants—which he'd used on a daily basis since returning from Wisconsin. And no one was going to tell him he had no right to buy the condominium, when it was good for Kyle to be in a home that he'd frequented when Ian was alive, that he was familiar with.

Fastening Kyle into the car seat in the rear of his Dodge Durango, Dante sped off to Tot Time. When he arrived, Kyle was sound asleep, his head tipped to the side.

"Come on, buddy, time to go," he lifted him out of the seat and carried him to his classroom, the smells of antiseptic mingled with bad diapers making him dizzy.

Katie Simms cringed when she saw them coming. Since Kyle's mother had passed away, he'd been a holy terror, especially during the drop-off phase. "Hi," she whispered, praying Kyle wouldn't awaken.

"Katie," Dante briefly scanned the middle-aged woman, her gray-streaked hair cropped short, and her plump body swimming in a smock. She wasn't a substitute mother by any means, but she was good with Kyle. "How are you today?"

"Oh, fine," she continued to hold her voice low. "Oversleep again?"

He rolled his eyes. "The little rascal kept me up all night. Sorry."

"No problem," she assured Dante, leading him to Kyle's own special crib in the back corner. "Just lie him gently down and be on your way."

When he slowly lowered Kyle into the crib, his eyes fluttered open and he glanced around the room, a panicked look crossing his face. The whining began as usual. "No!," he screamed. "No!"

"Shhh," Dante soothed, leaning into the crib to rub his back. "Just go back to sleep, Kyle."

Kyle let out an ear-piercing scream, and flipped onto his back. Throwing his head from side to side, he began stomping the surface of the mattress, screeching like a wildcat.

"Kyle, that's enough, now!" Dante warned, gripping the crib. "We can't go through this every day."

"No, no, no!" Kyle insisted, his face turning bright red, his nose beginning to drip with mucus.

"Kyle, I have to go…" Dante stepped from the crib and inched himself further away. Turning to Katie, he shouted over Kyle's screams, "Again, I'm sorry, but I have to get going. I have to be in court by eleven."

"It's all right," Katie assured him as she did every day. "The sooner you leave, the sooner he'll calm down." *Hopefully.*

Dante nodded his understanding and made his way to the door. Across the room, he could hear Kyle shrieking, "Hate you, Don-tee! Hate you! Want Bran-ma, want Bran-ma!"

With resentment, he knew precisely who 'Bran-ma' was. And he'd be damned if he'd give in to Brandy's legal demands and be separated from Kyle by hours of driving, even if the kid could be a little monster at times.

He hates me for leaving him, Dante thought painfully, as he pulled from the parking lot and turned toward the office. But how am I supposed to be with him all the time? I have a job I need to help support him. So how do you explain that to a child not yet two?

I'll take good care of him while you're working in Chicago, Brandy had said. Yeah, he snorted, ignoring a stab of guilt. Just like you took care of your own little brother.

Well, Kyle belonged with him. Kyle was comfortable with his Don-tee, had known him since birth. How could he go for days, even weeks, without seeing the little beast, despite the fact that he was a major handful to raise? And worse yet, how could he deposit the child in a strange home with a woman who'd once been negligent against her own brother?

And a woman who was obviously still in love with her dead husband.

It wasn't the answer. And he'd fight her petition for custody tooth and nail, never mind the fact that he couldn't get the sight, the smell, the taste of her out of his mind.

Maybe, just maybe, though, it *was* time for a change. After all, keeping a close watch on the enemy's every move was the best defense in his legal experience, he told himself, shoving aside the sense of anticipation that suddenly assaulted him.

So for the first time since buying the cottage next door to the inn, he felt like it had been the wisest decision he'd made in some time. He'd contacted the listing agent just prior to Julie's passing. In spite of a nagging guilt that had eaten away at him, he'd put a contract down on the property and recently finalized the sale. If anything, he'd rationalized all those weeks ago, that it was done simply to further expand Kyle's inheritance. The estates bordered one another, so what a better way to add to his holdings, and thus Kyle's future security, something he and Julie had never had?

There was no other reason, he assured himself, to have purchased the small bit of acreage. None, other than for his nephew's future.

Yes, it was time to nudge plan B into effect, and time to show that woman that she would never be able to take Kyle from him, regardless of the crafty lawyer she'd hired.

Plucking up his cell phone from the passenger's seat, he made the first call of many that day to further padlock his case and his strategy against Brandy MacKay.

❦   ❦   ❦

Christmas was approaching, and with it, the arrival of Maxine Hart. Brandy ignored the knots twisting tightly in her stomach as she checked the Martins out of suite number two.

"It was a lovely stay, darling," Melba Martin chimed, reaching across the office countertop to pat Brandy's hand. "We'll call in the spring for reservations for our fiftieth wedding anniversary," she beamed, her moon-shaped face flushing as she glanced up at her husband.

"Yeah," Pete Martin returned his wife's sentiments, pulling her bulky form against his tall, lanky one. "Fifty years with anyone seems crazy, don't it? But I'll stay a little longer with her just to be able to come back and sample those scrumptious cinnamon rolls of yours, Mrs. MacKay," he winked across the desktop, his hazel eyes twinkling below white bushy eyebrows.

"Yes, dear," Melba agreed. "Is there any chance we could get that recipe from you?"

"Well…" Brandy stalled. "If I gave you my old spy secrets, I may just have to kill you."

Pete threw his head back and cackled. "And we wouldn't want that now, would we? 'Cause then we wouldn't be able to celebrate our fiftieth."

"Yep, you got it," Brandy slapped the ledge, giving the subject finality. "Now you two have a safe trip back to Kansas, you hear?"

They turned and waved, Melba waddling her large girth across the foyer, Pete with his long arm draped about her as they left the faint scent of moth balls and cheap perfume behind. Brandy grinned, peering through the office window as they pulled away in their old model Thunderbird. How wonderful to be so in love that you'd put up with someone for fifty years, Brandy mused, suddenly feeling pensive, old, alone.

No, twenty-eight wasn't old by any means, but she'd always assumed that by now, she'd have a loving husband, kids, a dog, a house in the suburbs. Glancing around at the place that was now home, she examined the spacious office, the elegant foyer beyond, the long hallway that led to the recreation and dining areas, and the stairs rising to the private suites above, suites that were chameleon, in a sense, transforming from a romantic getaway, to a hideaway for a hermit.

Her quarters were home, yes, but an empty nest. Natalie had been moved down to her spare bedroom in her private quarters when occupancy had picked up recently, but somehow, she still felt alone, could still hear the giggles of an impish little boy with wide cobalt eyes and hair the color of Dante's, hair like thick black silk. Inhaling, she could smell the scent of him, a mixture of baby lotion, fabric softener, and sugar. He'd loved her desserts, Brandy smiled, recalling how Dante would take him into the kitchen and raid the dessert cooler.

"Brandy, honey," Natalie, approaching from the foyer side of the counter, waved a hand before Brandy's catatonic face. "You're thinking of that baby again, aren't you?"

Brandy's eyes refocused on her sister. "I can't help it, Nat," she sighed. "I know I could make him a good home here. A child's what this place needs. So why can't Dante see that?"

Natalie reached for Brandy's hand. "Go to him, Brandy. Just go. You've been agonizing over this for weeks now."

She snatched her hand away, turning to pace the office where she'd already worn a path on the varnished surface. "Sol tells me it's best to stay away. Until after the hearing when we see which direction things are headed."

"Sol's in this for the money. It's his *job*, for heaven's sake! But there are real people involved here with real feelings. You need to talk this out like civilized, healthy individuals."

It sounded so clinical, and yet, so sensible. Should she jeopardize her case by attempting to see them?

And she knew it wasn't just little Kyle she was yearning to see...

She couldn't get those hands out of her memory, the sensation of them, the hard, rough texture, exploring her body intimately, his hot kisses sizzling a path behind those very hands. The feel of his sculpted body on her, in her. The smoldering gold of his eyes as they seared her, daring her to resist, begging her not to.

"I've got the hang of this place," Natalie jolted Brandy out of her erotic thoughts. Running a hand through her loose rich, auburn hair, she coaxed, "Between Boomer and I, and the other help, we can handle things with you gone a couple days."

"But the Sandafords will be arriving soon, and that writer's finally coming to finish her manuscript, not to mention the—"

"Brandy!" Natalie scolded, slipping through the office door and taking her sister by the shoulders. "Will you listen to yourself? You sound like Max, like you think I'm not responsible enough."

"No!" Brandy shook her head, looking deep into her sister's smoky eyes. "Don't you *ever* compare me to her."

Natalie's lips thinned. "Then go, Brandy. Go and take care of this mess before it gets eaten alive by lawyers."

"I second that motion," Boomer strolled into the office, perching himself on the corner of Brandy's desk. "Lawyers are a lot like doctors. Their rates are as big as their egos."

Natalie turned narrowed eyes on him. She'd been putting up with his crap for several weeks now, and had just about had it. "Why don't you go back to the streets where you came from?"

Brandy gasped. "Natalie!"

Boomer directed his words at Brandy, yet kept his gaze glued to Natalie. "It's okay, Brandy. I've taken a lot worse from *the streets* than this. And Her Highness sure couldn't survive a minute where I came from," No, not all dolled up in her yellow cashmere sweater and tight slacks, and now, of all things, wearing her hair down like some carefree bimbo. He simply seethed inside, unable to disengage his eyes from her.

"What's going on here?" Brandy demanded, stepping between them "You two always seem to be snapping at each other."

They both remained speechless, like two school children being reprimanded, standing on either side of the principal.

"Well?" Brandy's voice rose as she crossed her arms, her eyes bouncing back and forth between the two.

"Ever since I met him," Natalie finally spoke up, "he's been like this toward me. Ask *him* why."

Brandy swung her heated gaze to her employee. "Boomer?"

Boomer slid from the desk and unfolded all six-foot-four of himself. "God, I'm sorry, Brandy. I…don't know why she gets my goat. It's—it's my fault."

"This isn't a playground, Boomer. I'm running a business here. You've always showed respect to everyone…until my sister arrived."

Natalie remained still, every ounce of her training willing her to keep her mouth shut.

"Yes, ma'am," Boomer nodded his head, a faint flush soaking the tan of his face. "I'm sorry. It won't happen again."

"Okay," Brandy finalized her part in this little skirmish. "I'm leaving now. I'm going into town to run by Sol's office, and then to pick up a few supplies. I'll have my cell phone. Now I suggest this problem get solved by the time I return." With that, she exited the office and left them to glare at one another.

"Well?" Natalie prompted softly, taking in the massive size of him, the way his scarred olive skin lent him the look of a roguish pirate, the way his broad shoulders cut to narrow hips and thick, strong legs. He was all man, all powerful, intimidating, yet breathtaking.

Boomer rolled his eyes, then sighed, stepping nearer, closing the wide gap between them. He took in the faint wariness in her magnetic pale blue eyes, the way she subtly flinched when he neared. "I won't hurt you," he said softly.

"I know." And she did. His eyes had dropped their menacing glare and had softened to a gentle brown. He stared at her now, as if he were memorizing every feature.

He lifted a hand to her hair, rubbed a lock between thumb and forefinger, then dropped his hand to his side. "I'm...sorry."

"Apology accepted," Natalie presented him with a warm smile, her heart-shaped lips thinning to reveal sparkling white teeth.

"It's just that..."

"Yes?" Now that the barrier was cracked, Natalie was able to switch to doctor mode. "Go on."

"You remind me so much of Rachelle's mother. She had the potential to be successful like you, but..."

"She went another route?" Natalie offered, encouraging patient to open up to doctor.

"Yes," he breathed. "She took the deadly road."

Natalie's hand came up to rest upon his hard chest. "Oh, Boomer. I'm so sorry. I had no idea."

Boomer looked down at her hand, then reached for it, studying the soft, slim length, the painted nails. "She'd wanted to be a doctor, like you," he traced his fingertip across the lines of her palm.

Natalie experienced a surge that traveled from her hand to her womb, and went straight into her heart. She watched him intently as he went on to explain his antipathy toward her.

"I had made a vow to get out of the inner city gang I was in, so I could support her and help her achieve her dreams, you see?"

Natalie nodded, feeling a wave of compassion for this man whom she'd have sworn only thirty minutes ago, was her enemy. His rich, deep voice touched her soul, her heart.

"But she couldn't get off that damn stuff. While I worked hard to make a life for her and Rachelle, she went to college by day, and took my hard-earned money to cop a hit by night. When they found her, her face was covered in a white powder—coke, of course—and her backpack was still on her back."

She just couldn't take it anymore, especially after the fire rushed up her arm and through her veins. Wrenching her hand from his, she threw herself against his brick-hard chest. "Oh, Boomer," she cried, her eyes filling with tears for him. "I'm so sorry for you, so very sorry!"

At first, he held his arms apart, looking down at the knock-out of a woman that was clinging to him, crying for *him*. But the incredulity quickly turned to desperate passion as his bear arms clamped around her.

He sighed heavily, inhaled the scent of her as she rested her head against the swell of his chest. "Natalie, I'm…I'm so sorry that I've been acting like such an ass."

"No," Natalie violently shook her head against him, her voice muffled. "Please. I understand."

He clasped her tightly to him, a warm relief flooding him.

They stood there for an eternity, locked in a desperate embrace, before he asked hesitantly, "Would you do me a favor, then?"

Tipping her head back to stare into his warm chocolate eyes, Natalie breathed, "Anything."

"Come to dinner at my house. Meet Rachelle. Tonight. I'll get Pedro to cover for a couple hours."

A warm glow began to spread through her. Her gray eyes blinked in wonder. "You—you mean it?"

"More than anything."

"You got yourself a deal, Boomer Ludwick," Natalie whispered, placing her hands lightly on his cheeks. With an instinct, and a sudden carnal urge, she raised on tip-toe and planted a soft kiss on his stunned lips.

"Now, I have to get back to work," she purred, backing slowly away, her gaze never leaving his as she sashayed from the office.

Boomer's eyes followed her until she slipped from view. Shaking the fog from his brain, he groaned inwardly. He didn't think that was quite what his boss had had in mind.

❧   ❧   ❧

"Have you thought of anything more we can use as ammo?" Sol asked, rubbing his palms together greedily. He was in his early sixties, a silver halo about his balding head, and thick bug-eyed lenses perched on his pug nose. Despite the fact that he was a small-town lawyer, he was dressed impeccably in a tailored suit with a silk tie, starched white shirt, and solid gold cuff lengths. He was obviously a very successful attorney, but Brandy reserved judgment for the day Kyle was under her roof.

"No. Just that his sister had said something in private to Dante right before she passed away," Brandy replied, seated before him in a wing-backed chair.

He rolled his chair up closer to the huge mahogany desk. Shaking a jeweled finger at her, he demanded, "What do you mean, 'private?'"

Brandy wrung her hands. "Look, I don't feel right about dragging what she said into this. She was on her deathbed."

"Do you want custody or not?" Sol leaned forward, planting his elbows over the paperwork of the very case he was now obsessed with. Thick silver brows drew together into one large eyebrow.

"Well, yes, but…but—"

"Mrs. MacKay," Sol breathed heavily and peeled his thick glasses from his flushed face. Twisting the spectacles between thumb and forefinger, he leaned back into his leather executive chair and rocked idly. "I get this a lot. Hesitation. Not wanting to hurt the other party. Now, that's all fine and proper for polite society, but this is an adoption or custody battle. And I'll be quite frank with you. Your chances don't look too good if we can't come up with some, as yet, uncovered detail that may sway the judge into feeling that you have at least the right to visitation or partial custody."

Studying her clasped hands in her lap, Brandy let his words soak into her conscience. Of course she wanted visitation, or custody of some form, but she didn't want to dredge up painful memories for Dante. There'd been that private exchange of words on Julie's death-bed, but what she'd meant, only Dante knew. And only a judge—an authority figure of the very judicial system Dante stood for in his profession—could require that he divulge what Julie had entrusted to him.

She looked up into the ruthless hazel eyes. "Oh, all right. I'll explain it to you."

Sol returned his glasses to his nose, a satisfied gleam magnified behind the lenses. Picking up his Mont Blanc pen, he perched it over the notepad. "Now, go on."

"It was when she was close to…to…you know, dying."

Sol nodded, all the while keeping his eyes on paper as he tran-scribed her words.

"It was like she was reminding him of something they'd dis-cussed—agreed to—at another time. She said only he knew what she really wanted for Kyle, or something like that."

"What do you think it was that she really wanted for her son?" Sol delved deeper, his pen scratching frantically on paper.

"Well, she'd already told me she wanted me to adopt Kyle. It was like she was making him promise to carry out her adoption wishes. Only he's not doing it, if that is, in fact, what she'd made him prom-ise. He's dragging Kyle out of bed every morning, taking him to a chaotic environment with dozens of other kids, when he could be with me, being loved and cared for and given undivided attention almost every minute of every day."

"I think," she went on after a thoughtful pause, "that they had some sort of agreement or that he promised her something—I don't know what—in regard to Kyle's future. Somehow, I have this distinct feeling that it has to do with me, with the three of us."

Sol dropped the pen onto the stack of papers and leaned back in his chair, clasping his hands behind his head. With a smug grin, he said, "Well, looks like this might be the piece of information that could sway the judge. Mr. Saxon is a man of the law. If things progress to a trial, we'll get him on the stand, and under oath, he'll be forced to reveal what his sister had entrusted him with."

"And if it's not in my favor, or if he lies or pleads to the fifth?" Brandy asked, her heart thumping loudly in her chest.

Sol's smile faded. "Then your chances are probably nil."

Go to him, Natalie had urged her. Was that the answer, to corner him, entice him? "What if I go to him and try to…coax it out of him? To see if there's more to their pact?"

He shook his head vehemently. "No. Don't jeopardize the case by getting further involved," Sol advised, waving a hand.

"I want to see him," Brandy leaned closer to Sol's desk, placing her hands against the front rim of it. 'Him,' though, she knew included them both.

Sol leaned in too, placing his hands in much the same manner as she had. "*I said no*. It's too risky."

Brandy cleared her throat. "Mr. Carver. Am I not paying *you*?"

His lips curled derisively. "Of course."

"Then I direct the show, here. I'm paying for your advice and your expertise in litigation. But I know Dante, and I feel that a meeting with him would be beneficial for both sides, and mostly for little Kyle."

Sol shook his head and sighed. "It's your money. The fee will stand, even if you blow it."

Brandy clamped her jaw and leaped to her feet, and for one split second, Sol flinched. "You'll get your filthy money, Mr. Carver, whether we solve the problem in or out of court. But I want to handle this my way. You just keep doing your paper shuffling and snitch hiring, and I'll head on down to Chicago and see what I can find out. Agreed?"

Nostrils flaring, Sol rose. "Of course, Mrs. MacKay. You understand my position, though, I'm sure. But as you've said, you will pay me my *filthy* money no matter what, so, have it your way. Now, if you'll excuse me, it's time for my next appointment."

"What I understand, Mr. Carver," Brandy tilted in slowly, slapping her palms on the files laying open on his desktop, "is that you aren't the only lawyer in this world. I have no qualms about finding one who seems to suite my needs better than you do."

Sol shifted his feet behind the desk. He desperately wanted to keep this connection going with Dante Saxon's case. If he couldn't have the young man working *for* him, he at least wanted to best him in court. "Now, let's not get too hasty here, Mrs. MacKay. We can work things out. If you feel seeing Mr. Saxon may help, then you have my blessing."

Brandy straightened and flipped her purse strap onto her shoulder. "Now you're talking."

Sol grinned accommodatingly and rounded his desk, coming to extend his hand to her. "Good. Good. Then you get in touch with me when you return, let me know if you get any information helpful to the case."

Brandy limply shook his hand, then crossed the richly carpeted floor to exit his office. Over her shoulder, she replied cheerily, "Keep up the good work, Mr. Carver. The meter is ticking."

CHAPTER 11

"Kyle!" Dante's voice boomed through the condominium. "You get your little butt down from there right now!" Was he ever going to get any work done?

Kyle's mischievous grin appeared with a bubbly giggle as he tight-roped across the back of the sofa, teetering precariously form side to side.

"Kyle!" Dante growled, throwing down his pen. He'd been trying to prepare for tomorrow's case of two son's battling over their deceased wealthy father's estate. He was representing the son who'd cared for his ailing father for the last decade. The other son had run off to Europe and blown his entire inheritance, and now disputed his father's will, siting childhood abuse.

When the phone rang, he swiped Kyle just before he tumbled from the back of the high sofa, then plucked up the cordless. "Hello?" he barked, out of breath.

"Dante?"

At the sweet, familiar voice, he held in a breath. A mental image of her golden beauty appeared before him. "Brandy? Is that you?"

"Yes, I…" her heart fluttered at the sound of his voice. "I was surprised to see that you'd registered at the inn under Ian's old address."

Dante paused briefly, shoving the guilt aside. "Ah, yes, I was the one who bought his condo. I did it for Kyle. He's familiar with the place."

Brandy nodded, swallowing a burning lump. "I—I understand. I was just surprised." *And feeling a bit betrayed,* she told herself.

God, it was good to hear her voice! "Is everything okay?" Dante asked, suddenly aware of the strained tone in her voice.

"Well, yes," she hesitated. "But I need to see you."

Kyle squirmed on his hip, and he bent to set him safely on the floor. "Brandy, you know that's not a good idea…"

"Dante, please," she begged. "You left so abruptly after…Julie… We didn't have a chance to try and work this out."

"It will all get worked out in court, you know that," he breathed, his lids closing as he hated his own words. Damn, he wished she were here, wished he could grant her every request.

"Dante, please…" her voice cracked softly, and he could swear he could hear the sound of her tears trickling down her smooth cheeks, trailing from the glistening lime-green of her eyes.

"Brandy…" he warned, unable to scold any further, yearning to hold her, as he'd yearned every day since leaving Wisconsin weeks ago.

"I'm coming up," she sniffled in his ear, bringing finality and firmness to her words.

"Coming up? You mean you're here?"

"Please, just give the receptionist the okay. She's sitting here waiting to take the phone from me." He heard the shuffle as the phone traded hands. She wasn't going to give him further opportunity to deny her. And he knew he wasn't going to give himself a chance to deny her either.

"Mr. Saxon?" came the nasally voice. "Should I give Mrs. MacKay an elevator card?"

Dante's partner and lawyer in the custody case would blow his top. If Martin Drew knew he was about to be in close contact with the other party of litigation, he'd probably drop his case and refuse to represent him. But he wouldn't find out. "Yes, Mitzy. Send her up."

Mitzy slid an elevator card across the desk, her blood-red nails scraping the laminated surface. "Take the elevator to the fifth floor—"

"I know where it is," Brandy cut her off gently, then turned toward the elevator.

Mitzy lifted a slim shoulder. Hell, Mr. MacKay's old apartment had always had a revolving door. Now that Julie had passed away, and her brother had bought Ian's condo, and he now took care of her son….and…was that right? Or was he Julie's cousin? Whatever. I just don't have time for this petty gossip, Mitzy snorted silently, clicking sculpted nails against the phone panel to answer an incoming call.

Brandy pressed the buzzer outside Dante's door, ignoring the feeling of déjà vu. When the door swung open, Brandy thought her heart had stopped. He was dressed in khakis with a white dress shirt unbuttoned and hanging open, and a white undershirt pulled haphazardly from his pants. His dark hair was mussed, as if he'd been pulling at it in frustration, while a five o'clock shadow completed the dashing look. His eyes, a soft brown, seemed to etch her from head to toe. A thrill went through her, flames licking at her loins, as his eyes caressed her, savored her.

Holding the door open with one hand, the other planted casually on his hip, he said huskily, "Brandy."

Damn, but she was the image of sexuality itself, standing there in leather boots, snug jeans, and a white silk blouse unbuttoned to just above the shadow of her cleavage. A brown leather jacket hung open over the blouse, and somehow emphasized those luscious breasts, outlining them as they heaved up and down with her rapid breathing. She wore her hair long, and had recently had it trimmed, soft layers here and there framing her arresting face. Green eyes sparkled with a mixture of indecision and determination, while her lips pursed into a stubborn pink—kissable—O. The entire package was an unfair assault on his libido, and he was suddenly grateful that he'd kept his undershirt hanging outside of his pants.

"Dante," she breathed, breathless from the hurried walk up the hall. The closer she'd gotten, the faster her legs had pumped.

"Bran-ma!" came a tiny voice from inside. "Bran-ma!" Kyle raced up the long foyer hall.

"Kyle—" Dante shoved a hand through his hair in frustration as Kyle hurtled toward her.

When Brandy saw him, her heart twisted painfully. God, how he'd grown! Dropping her purse to the floor, she squatted down and opened her arms wide. "Kyle!"

When he threw himself against her, she felt her maternal hormones surge. He smelled of baby lotion, ketchup, and just plain Kyle. It was a scent that she would bottle if she could. His little body clung to her, and she savored the softness, the warmth, the sound of his labored breathing as he squeezed her with excitement.

Kissing his chubby cheek, she pulled him far enough away to look into those soft blue eyes. Lord, he looked so much like Dante... "I missed you, sweetie," she kissed his other cheek.

"Missed you, Bran-ma," Kyle placed his tiny hands on her cheeks and kissed her square on the mouth.

Delighted, Brandy scooped him closer and stood to stare into wary flaming eyes. "Dante. May I come in?"

"Do I have a choice?" he nearly snarled, stepping aside to allow her to enter.

"No," she said bravely, marching into the apartment she knew well. But when she reached the living area, the place where she'd visited on occasion with Ian, she halted in shock.

It was now more a comfortable den than the elegant sitting room it used to be. The floor plan was the same, of course, but Dante had totally redecorated. The floors had been stripped of carpeting, revealing the rich hardwood that had been hidden below it. A new mantle, a thick ornately carved oak, was now perched over the fireplace lined with Christmas garland. The furniture was in deep, overstuffed plaids of green, brown, navy, and maroon. Gone were the elegant drapes, having been replaced with simple vertical blinds. The walls were painted a deep cream and accented by an oak chair rail, below it a hunter green wallpaper pattern. The chandelier had been replaced by a ceiling fan, and ceramic lamps sat atop scattered oak end tables. And there in the far corner was a modest Christmas tree ornamented haphazardly.

"Wow," she sang, her eyes darting around happily. "I like it. It's...cozy."

"Thanks. I let Kyle choose where to hang the tree ornaments." He unknowingly breathed a sigh of relief. "As far as the room itself, I like to be comfortable, not stuffy."

Brandy turned, Kyle perched on her hip, and granted him a sunny smile. "Ian was stuffy, wasn't he?"

"Daddy?" Kyle asked suddenly, as if he'd forgotten, until now, that Ian had existed.

Dante reached for him, plucking him from Brandy's tight grip. "Yes, you little beast. Now, it's nite-nite time for you," he said as Kyle growled, imitating the Lion King.

"No!" Brandy placed a hand on Dante's arm. "Could I please hold him a little longer?"

Her hand, warm and gentle, soft against the taut muscle of his forearm, burned like hell.

"He really should get to bed. And I have tons of work before I can get some sleep."

"Can I help you get him ready for bed, then?" she asked, her eyes lighting with a hopeful glow.

God, he wished she wouldn't look at him that way, all sad-eyed and...sexy, all at the same time. Damn her, anyway. "Sure," he relented, instinct telling him this was a terrible mistake.

Remember, Dante, his own voice reverberated in his head. *This is the woman who's seeking custody of Kyle, the woman who wants to take him away from you.*

She wanted to throw her arms around him in gratitude—and to feel his hard body against hers again. As she followed him into the bedroom, the bedroom that was once Ian's office, but was now converted into a toddler's room, complete with its sports theme and scattered toys, she knew what she was going to do to rectify this situation.

And the solution wasn't restricted to just talking, as originally planned…

"Oh, I forgot a sippy cup—he always has chocolate milk at bedtime," Dante mumbled. Plopping Kyle down on the bed carved into a miniature race car, he turned to her and asked, "Would you watch him while I go get it?"

"I'd love to," she smiled warmly, floating across the room to sit next to Kyle on the race car bed.

Dante slipped from the room, shooting a cautious look over his shoulder.

"Now, let's see," Brandy glanced around the bedroom, her eyes resting on a diaper bag. "You'll need a dry diaper before getting into bed. And some snuggly jammies." She'd taken very good care of Brian, and had known all the rituals of preparing a toddler for bed.

But she'd mistakenly taken her eyes off Brian for just thirty seconds…

"Jammies?" Kyle's tiny voice interrupted her thoughts, his voice growing husky with a sudden wave of exhaustion, his eyelids becoming heavy.

"Yes, honey," Brandy searched the drawers of a multicolored chest and found pajamas with enclosed feet and snaps to hold everything together. Reaching for a diaper, she returned to Kyle and began undressing him.

"You're tired, aren't you, sweetie?" she asked gently, expertly undressing him, then slipping his arms into the pajama shirt, snapping it up the front. Unfastening the diaper, she placed a new one under his bottom and wiped his skin with a moist baby wipe before taping the new diaper in place. Slipping his legs into the footsies, she connected the remainder of the suit and lifted his limp body into her arms. Crossing to a wooden rocker, she carefully lowered herself into it, and tucked Kyle over her chest.

And sighed.

Rocking smoothly, she hummed softly, rubbing her hand over his back. His breathing became regular, and she hugged him closely, closing her eyes as the warmth of him permeated her heart.

And she began to hum a lullaby to him, a tune that'd been buried in her subconscious for fifteen long years.

"How'd you do that?" Dante asked quietly, leaning against the door frame. He'd been watching her effortlessly care for Kyle, lovingly touching, dressing, rocking him. And the sight had caused him a mixture of guilt, annoyance, and a curious tenderness. He could feel the custody case slipping from him, could almost feel himself handing Kyle over voluntarily.

She was good with him. Too good.

Eyes flying open to see Dante tilted lazily against the doorway, a full sippy cup of chocolate milk clutched in his hand, she whispered, "Do what?"

"Get him so easily to sleep," Dante supplied, coming into the room to squat before the rocker. "He never goes to sleep that quickly for me."

She lifted her free shoulder. "Just did what a mom does."

Her words were meant to imply that she was capable of custody, but he didn't bite. "Well, let me put him in bed now. I have lots of work ahead of me."

"And we need to talk yet," she warned, rising carefully and placing Kyle tenderly on his pillow as Dante lowered the covers. Drawing the blankets up, she tucked him in and kissed his warm cheek.

Dante again ignored the affectionate motherly care. "Brandy, I really don't have time to have a long discussion with you. And we really should be letting our lawyers handle this."

Brandy placed a stuffed bear under Kyle's slack arm, then briskly left the room and returned to the den. It was a comfortable, more masculine room, she surmised, dropping to the sofa and folding her legs under her. Patiently, she waited for Dante to follow.

"Brandy..." his voice was deep, edged with an omen of darkness.

Without turning toward him, she reached for the remote and switched on the television, scanning the channels until she found the Discovery channel in which it featured the mating call of wolves. "I'm not leaving until we're done discussing this. You left so bluntly. I had no idea you were going to leave so soon after the funeral. And I was trying so hard to give you time to mourn, to not burden you with extra baggage. I want to see for myself how you're faring, how little Kyle's doing. Can't you understand that?"

Dante fought the urge to go to her, to kiss her silly until she'd listen to reason. "I'm sorry, but I have a life that I needed to get on with. I'd already put my job on hold for weeks just by bringing her to the inn to die."

Eyes suddenly filling with tears, Brandy finally turned to look at him as he stood like an uncomfortable stranger in his own home. "But you didn't have to be so cruel about it. You didn't have to take him so abruptly from me, Dante. I've missed him so much...and I've missed you, too."

Her words sliced right through his gut. Closing his eyes briefly in denial, he expelled a breath, then came to sit next to her on the sofa. If only she didn't still pine over her dead husband, if only she were more trustworthy, if only he didn't have so much to lose...

"Brandy, please. Don't do this. We're both living two separate lives. Hours apart. I don't want to split Kyle in two."

"Neither do I, Dante," her eyes glittered into green pools. "But I love him. I know it sounds crazy, but I do. I feel like he's my son, like I'm being denied my right to mother him. Please. Can't you understand that?"

He did, because he felt like he was Kyle's father, but he'd been in Kyle's life from day one. He had a valid reason to feel that way. Reaching up to wipe a tear from her cheek, he kept his hand there as she nuzzled it. Tamping down the jolt of heat that raced through his veins, he said, "I have to do what's right for Kyle. I have to think of him, above all else."

"But Julie *wanted* me to adopt him. She begged me to," Brandy appealed beseeching eyes to him, the soft feminine scent of her rising to assault him before he was aware of it.

"Julie was trying to alleviate her own guilt toward you. Ian told her you couldn't have children. And she thought a child should have a mother before a father...because she never had a mother to love her."

"Her guilt has given me hope," she vowed, squeezing his hand to emphasize her words. But Julie and Ian weren't the subject here. In fact, their names went right over her head. "Before she passed away, she said something to you..."

Dante snatched his hand from her, then rose to pace before the cold fireplace. "Don't go there, Brandy," he advised her menacingly.

"What was it?" she begged, rising, then crossing the room to plant her feet before him. "What was it that she said you knew? She said that only you knew what she wanted for Kyle. Besides my adopting him, what was her dying wish, Dante? Did it, too, involve me?"

Presenting her his profile, he placed both hands on the mantle and leaned against it, as if he were bracing the wall against a strong force.

"Dante?" she repeated, placing a firm hand upon his shoulder. "Are you listening to me?"

Looking up at the ceiling, he suddenly purged his system, blurting out, "She wanted you and I to come together as Kyle's parents. To marry. It was a crazy, lunatic brainstorm of hers that she harped on for months. 'I'm only thinking of Kyle's future,' she'd always say. But," he turned his back to her, throwing his hands up in the air. "I can be both a father and a mother to him. She never had that faith in me. I don't need a wife to be able to take care of him."

"Was that what had you turning tail and running?" Brandy asked, her voice bubbling with humor.

Dante whirled, his eyes transformed to near slits. "You think that's funny?"

"Well, yes," she wiped away tears of laughter. "Considering I'm technically not out of the mourning period anyway, and the last thing a widow wants is another husband." *At least most widows.*

Feeling suddenly foolish, he ran a shaky hand through his mussed hair. "I know that," he insisted.

Her smile faded. "But I wouldn't mind," she came one step closer, setting her hand like a brand on his chest, "being your lover." She was a woman who suddenly knew exactly what she wanted. She no longer cared that he'd deceived her, no longer cared that he'd played a role in keeping her in the dark all those years ago during Ian's affair with Julie. She knew this man, and she knew that he'd done it all for the love of a sister, for Kyle and even, in an odd way, for herself.

Dante swallowed hard, instinctively taking one step back. "W-what?"

Her eyes, sharp green arrows, were honing in on him, marking their target. Dante suddenly felt much like a bull's eye, standing erect, yet out there in the open waiting vulnerably to be pierced by the swift flight of twin green arrows.

"I've missed you," she said boldly, making up for the dis-tance—and the wasted time they'd spent apart—as she reached to place both hands on his chest. "The inn seems so…vacant without you there."

His head was spinning with the fragrance of her, the hot imprints of her hands marking him indelibly as hers. She was licking her lips, the merciless cat eyeing her delicious prey, stalking, needing, craving.

Fool suddenly turned genius, he halted his retreat. How could he combat such feline loveliness? Hell, why was he even contemplating it?

With a guttural sound erupting from deep in his throat, Dante reached for her, the sudden panther turning on his quarry.

She didn't back down. Those days were over. Seeing the hunger spring to his blazing eyes, the way his body suddenly relaxed, moving fluidly, gracefully, she nearly panted with anticipation. Instead, she opened her arms to him, making room for his massive body, accepting him fully into her soul.

"I want you, Dante," she breathed, clinging to him, racing her lips up his neck until she found his lips, warm, surprised, hungry. *I love you*, she added silently.

"Brandy," he returned her kiss, sucking the very life from her, his hands moving frantically over her back, her firm rear, her sides. "Are you sure you want to complicate things? The custody case and all—"

Clamping her palm over his mouth, she whispered, "Shhh. Don't bring that into this. This is *our* time. I need you, and I think you need me too."

Her eyes were flaming emeralds, promising treasures of unlimited wealth. As he reached for her hand and pulled it gently from his mouth, he kissed the palm, his tongue snaking out to trace a path to her wrist. When he found her pulse, throbbing fast and hot, his eyes rose again to meet hers.

"Darling," he murmured quietly, recalling her early resistance to him all those weeks ago. "You surprise me."

She studied the yellow of his eyes, the keen panther, the way the fire in them made her feel deliciously chosen as his next victim. "I surprise myself," she agreed, pulling her wrist from his grip and clasping her hands at the back of his neck.

He glanced over at the dining table piled high with research books, documents, his briefcase. "I have so much work to do…" he groaned regrettably.

"Just thirty minutes," she begged, raising on tip-toe to capture his lips in an electrifying kiss. Against his mouth, she coaxed, "Then I'll go."

Thirty minutes. That was all she needed to convince him that this custody battle was detrimental to all three of them—and that Julie was right. They should be together. They should be a family. But convincing Dante, despite the hunger in his eyes, would be her greatest challenge yet. She would start with making love to him, love that he'd never be able to forget—in fact, would refuse to be without. Simply put, she would seduce him, prove to him that she did belong in their lives. Then she'd persuade him to let her take Kyle back to Wisconsin with her for a few days. Because Kyle would be her number one cheerleader, she was certain. He'd open his uncle's eyes to a reality that Dante was resisting.

And the reality was that she didn't want to be without the two loves of her life.

"Take me to your bed," she commanded, kneading his back, racing her hands under his shirt and around to explore the fine cords of his pectorals, then his biceps, flexed now in a mixture of restraint and expectation.

Her hands were hot, tempting bolts striking his loins with sizzling flames of fire. "Ah, Brandy. How can I turn that down?" he growled. Sweeping her up into his arms, he carried her to his bedroom. It was decorated just as comfortably and rustically as the living area, the unmade king-sized bed piled high with dark blankets and sheets.

But the room was the least of her concern. When he placed her on the bed, she wasted no time. Hurriedly, she shoved the heaps of blankets aside and stripped her clothing off, then held up her hands to him, welcoming him, urging him to come to her.

Dante shed his own garments, then stood looking down at her, mesmerized. Her eyes were glazed with an emotion he didn't care to name, and he felt his heart clenching painfully as she whispered, urging him to join her like a witch chanting, casting a spell upon him. Shimmering hair was fanned out around creamy shoulders, the slim column of her neck drawing his eyes to the perfect globes below. Her breasts were full, rising high with her heavy breathing, pink-tipped mountains waiting anxiously for his exploration. He studied her flat abdomen flowing gently into hips that rose and fell, gyrating even now, before he'd even touched her there. The golden triangle of her womanhood was nestled between her slim, firm thighs, raised now to support the thrust of her hips. His eyes rose reluctantly to, once again, absorb the pleading eyes, the pursed lips.

A goddess. That was the only term that even came close to describing her. With a moan, he moved closer, lowering himself to the bed.

Brandy was nearly breathless with the sight of him, all dark and handsome, his eyes searing her from head to toe. She'd previously likened him to Indian, panther, wolf, but now, now with his perfectly sculpted body above her, every muscle, every limb, erect and seeming to glide silkily toward her, he was a sleek black hawk in pursuit. Arms spread, descending on her, Brandy accepted this carnal destiny, welcomed the hawk as he spotted his mate and swooped in to stake his claim.

His journey was one of swift flight. Stretching out beside her, Dante reached frantically for her, nearly slamming her naked body flush with his. He rolled to his back, pulling her with him until she lay atop his hard chest. The last few weeks had been torture on his libido, and now, with her floating above him like an ethereal angel, he was in heaven.

"It's too late to change your mind," he warned, dragging her up and over the silk-encased steel hardness of his manhood. "I'm pain-fully hard with needing you."

At his words, Brandy experienced a flood of heat where his hard-ness probed at her soft warmth. "No," she nipped at his lower lip, "it's too late for *you*," she spread her legs and encased him in one fluid motion, "ah, to change your mind."

His eyes flew wide, as did hers, the sensation nearly enough to push them both over the edge. "Ohhh, Brandy," he groaned, hooking his fingers behind her neck to draw her mouth to his.

It was an urgent kiss, one of hunger and famine, a kiss that told of two lovers starving for that which they couldn't define in words. His tongue plundered her mouth, darting, circling, searching every recess of her. She accepted the exploration, and set out to reciprocate in kind, moving in a frantic rhythm over the silky hardness of him. He held fast to her, snaring her face in the vice of his hands, allowing her to drive at her own pace, her own tempo, over and over again.

Her hips rose and fell, completely impaling herself with him, but he could take the torture no more. His hands snaked down her back and gripped the softness of her buttocks, assisting her in a momen-tum that was fast bringing them to release, the muscles of his arms flexing with his urgent need.

"Dante…" she panted, splaying her hands over his taut pecs. "I—I," she moaned helplessly, needing to express the depth of her feelings for him, for them, for the future she realized at this very moment, that she wanted more desperately than she'd known before now.

Dante was looking up at her, the soft breasts bouncing above him, the slim waist flaring to hips that held him captive. In her eyes, he glimpsed their future, saw a complicated life that he refused to entwine with the tenderness that he was now feeling.

His words emphasized his denial. "Shhh, Brandy," he suddenly rolled with her, keeping himself easily inside her. When he came over her, he shoved his hands under her hips and lifted her to meet him. "No words. Show me how you feel with your body."

Had she not been near the brink of ecstasy, the dissent in his words would've pierced her heart. But she only wanted to soar with him, to reach that pinnacle that only Dante could take her to. So she led him to that place of exhilaration, the abode of her heart, her soul, her spirit, rising to meet him with the strength of a woman whose needs were her strength. They met together in heaven, and he took her to a corner of it that she'd never seen before. Soaring over clouds, mist, and into eternity, the hawk glided with his mate as they came together, shattering into a million pieces of white-hot stars against the dark of the night.

CHAPTER 12

She awoke to a delicious heat along her backside. But it was the bundle of warmth tucked into the front curve of her body as she lay on her side, that had her eyes slowly coming open. The dawn was just breaking, and Brandy could see the pale shafts of light filtering through the cracks of the blinds, bending gently over the little face. Somehow, in the quiet of the night, Kyle had sought her out, and she'd accepted him in sleep without reserve. Dante breathed softly in slumber at her backside, but it was Kyle who completed the circle of cozy love.

They were a family.

Her heart flipped, ceased beating, cautiously began thumping again. With a careful breath, lest she disturb the tranquility, she examined Kyle, memorized every curve of his profile, every dark lash that lay arched against his chubby cheek. His breathing was even, soft, in euphony with Dante's, and she watched, fascinated as his small pursed lips suckled in sleep, as if he dreamed of the security of a bottle in his mouth.

True, he was Ian's flesh and blood, but as he slept, lids closed against the blue of Ian's legacy, he was all Dante...and Julie. He'd inherited the Saxon likeness, the almond skin, the blue-black, sleek hair, the square jaw, and the irresistible magnetism that immediately brought Dante to mind. And in that instant, she realized that she'd never loved Ian. Oh, she'd thought she loved him back then, when he'd caught her up in his whirlwind lifestyle, but now, looking at his son, she knew that this was the only part of him that she loved.

Somehow in the recent past, she'd fallen in love with this little imp of a child, and in him, she could only see his uncle. As Dante stirred behind her, she closed her eyes, savoring the last few seconds of heaven. For how could she call it anything else, when the child she adored and the man she loved, cradled her in a bed of bliss?

"Oh, God," Dante mumbled, lifting his head to peek at the clock. "What time is it?"

Brandy rolled her head gently around, her breath catching at the rugged sight of him. "It's morning," she whispered.

Dante's head snapped around to her. Sleepy eyes widened with disbelief. *Oh shit!* he thought, sitting bolt upright in bed. *He'd blown the whole custody case!*

"What's the matter?" she placed a hand on his bare back, caressing the rippling muscles.

Dante leaped from the bed, standing in all his naked glory, mindless of nothing but the sight of the witch who'd seduced him and his nephew tucked closely against her. "What are you doing?" he accused, his eyes bouncing from her to Kyle and back again.

Jesus, he growled silently. *Why did they have to look so* right *together?*

Brandy remained still, loathe to disturb Kyle and the joy she'd felt at his closeness. "What do you mean, what am I doing? I'm lying here just as you were, and *trying not to wake Kyle*," she emphasized her words with a finger to her lips.

"Jesus, what have I done?" Dante began pacing, gripping his head with both hands—still naked. "Martin's going to have my head!"

"Martin?" Brandy looked to him, then to Kyle as he stirred. Yawning noisily, he crawled atop Brandy's chest, snuggling against Dante's T-shirt that she'd donned after the last round of lovemaking. Briefly, she held her arms out and stared down at him in wonder. Then, as if she'd come to her senses, she enfolded him tightly in her embrace and pulled the blankets up over his back.

Lord, it couldn't get anymore complicated, Dante's mind screamed, eyeing the picture she made, all sleepy golden softness embracing innocent—finally reticent—child. They were looking entirely too cozy.

Frustrated, he threw out, "He's my lawyer in the custody case. Brandy," he shook his head, reaching for a pair of boxer shorts and slipping them hastily on. "You've got to go. This shouldn't have happened."

Feeling only a vague disappointment that he'd covered himself, for the boxers were nearly as sexy as his nakedness, Brandy smiled slyly, "But it did."

Dante planted his hands on the bed, leaning menacingly toward her. "And it won't happen again."

Brandy swallowed a lump, then gently placed Kyle onto her pillow and tucked him in. Rising, she went in search of her clothes. "If that's the way you want it, fine."

"It's the way it should be," Dante sighed, watching her petite form bend to pick up her bra, her panties… Wrenching his eyes from the curve of her luscious bottom, peeking out from below his T-shirt, he growled, "And it's the way it *will* be."

"I said fine," she agreed, pulling the shirt over her head and standing naked before stepping into her white lace panties. "I'll be out of your hair as soon as I find my jeans."

Dante snatched them from under the bed, one lone leg peering out. "Here," he growled, tossing the denim over the bed to her side.

Slipping her socks on first, she then bent to slide her legs into the pants, then zipped them effortlessly over her flat belly. "Dante…" she said softly, searching for her blouse and jacket.

His eyes were drawn to her lush breasts, sitting full and pert above jeans and a narrow waist. Her hair hung in disarray about shoulders squared now in her proud stance. God, he was a fool!

"What?" he snarled.

Glancing over at Kyle's slumbering form, a small ball curled up under the covers that they'd recently shared, she asked, "Can I take him back with me—just for a few days?" Dante would come around, she just knew it. How could he not after the incredible love they'd shared last night?

"I have to get going," Dante avoided the question. "I had a ton of work to do last night…before you got here. I never got back to it—"

"Answer my question," she demanded, slipping on her bra and fastening it before sliding her arms into her silk blouse.

He exhaled heavily. "I refuse to pass him back and forth. He needs to stay put in one home."

Buttoning her blouse, Brandy rounded the bed and came to stand before his erect form. "Why? What's wrong with giving him the love of two people? Lots of kids live in two different households and turn out fine."

"Because!" Dante roared, flinging his hands up in the air. "I know what it's like being shuffled from home to home. And I refuse to put Kyle through that."

Brandy stuffed her blouse in her jeans and donned her leather jacket, then bent to slip her boots on. Rising, she placed a hand on Dante's heaving chest. "Dante," she began, clamping her gaze onto his hot one. "What you went through as a child, going from foster home to foster home, is not the same as this situation. We both love him. He'd be shared willingly by each of us, not neglected, as you and Julie were."

Dante stepped away from the brand of her hand, suppressing the flare of heat that shot to his loins. "Your viewpoint isn't going to change the facts, Brandy. He'll not be juggled between two homes. We live too far apart, and you know it."

Brandy left her hand suspended where he'd abandoned it, then slowly drew it back to her heart. "I'll fly here to escort him back with me, drive here to pick him up, do whatever it takes to see him. *Please,* Dante."

He didn't look at her again, didn't have to see her face to know the pain was written all over it. But again, he had to put Kyle first. "I can't trust you…"

"You what?" she shook her head, uncertain she'd heard right. "You can't trust me with him?" her voice rose an octave. "Is that what you were about to say?"

Dante remained silent, his eyes roaming the room, touching everything but her.

"Are you referring to my little brother, Brian?"

Dante's only answer was a sigh.

Her eyes glistened with unshed tears. *He knew about Brian's kidnapping.* "So, I assume Natalie's stuck her nose in things, just like my loving mother. Either that, or your lawyer, Martin what's-his-name, has a snoop in his employ. Well, I guess I deserved that," she choked. "I can't blame you for fearing it may happen again."

So, the court case was inevitable after all, she mused, furious with him. She took one last, longing look at Kyle, then spun on her heel and glided from the room.

Dante turned to be assaulted by the emptiness of the room, save for Kyle lying on the pillow that she'd vacated. Had he truly been referring to her brother, or had his mistrust been more in the fact that he felt her to still be in love with her deceased husband? Hell, since Brandy MacKay had been in his life, he didn't know what the hell he thought of anything! Picking up the alarm clock that'd failed to wake him that morning, he ripped it from the wall and flung it across the room, ruing the day Julie had ever gotten mixed up with Ian MacKay.

"You told him!" Brandy accused, slamming her keys down on the office counter, and piercing her sister with twin green bullets. She'd taken two more days of solace in a Chicago hotel before returning to Wisconsin. It was the least she could've done for her sister's safety.

Natalie hung the phone up; she'd just booked an entire wedding party for a weekend in March. Glancing warily at Boomer, who'd been preparing a bank deposit, Natalie asked, "Told who, what?"

"Dante," Brandy's expression was a mixture of pain and anger. "You told him about Brian."

Natalie paused, folding her hands on the counter in front of her. "Oh. That."

"Oh *that*?" Brandy asked incredulously. "That's all you can say?"

Natalie cleared her throat. "Honey, I'm sorry. I thought I was doing you a favor."

"Yes," Brandy's eyes dripped with venom. "You did me a huge favor, *Maxine*," she spat. "You cost me custody of Kyle!"

Natalie gasped, her auburn brows arching.

"Did I hear my name?" came a voice from the stairs.

Brandy spun around with lethal speed. She had no trouble locating the source of the familiar voice. There, standing like a regal queen, was her mother, Maxine Hart. A tall amazon woman, bright red hair cut in a severe bob, she floated down the last few stairs, and glided across the foyer with her chin held high. Dressed in a deep green tailored suit and adorned with diamonds and flashy gold, she resembled the glimmering Christmas tree that Brandy had erected days ago in the dining room.

"Hello, Brandy," she looked down her nose at her youngest daughter. "I finally found you."

Brandy pounded her fist on the overhang, while Natalie, standing on the opposite side of the office window, flinched. "Yes, Max," Brandy hissed. "Once again, you've hunted me down like an animal."

"And you've evaded me like a sly fox," Maxine replied with equally high volumes.

"Shhh," Boomer came forward. "Ladies. We have guests."

Brandy ignored her assistant, but heeded his words. "So you're here," she said in hushed tones. "Now what are you going to do?"

Maxine flung a slim hand up in the air and sang, "Why, spend Christmas with my children, of course."

Fa-la-la, Brandy thought grimly, grinding her teeth. "I take it you've been settled into one of my suites upstairs." *She better not be settled into my quarters,* she seethed inwardly, glancing suspiciously at Natalie.

A finely waxed brow rose as Maxine noted the possessive tone to her daughter's voice. "You needn't worry, dear. Natalie showed me to your suite number one upstairs."

Brandy gave her sister an apologetic glance, for suite number one was the farthest away from her own quarters, situated on the opposite side of the house above the guest living room. "Does it meet your needs?"

Maxine clicked her tongue and rolled her eyes. "Well, I would have preferred one with a fireplace and hot tub, but Natalie tells me those are reserved."

"Yes, they are," Brandy's eyes softened further on her sister. Unless they'd booked more reservations while she'd been in Chicago, that had been a surprising outright lie coming from Natalie.

"Maybe when your guests leave…" Maxine suggested, tapping perfectly manicured nails on the countertop near Brandy, her blue-green, thickly painted eyes sparkling expectantly.

Brandy took two small steps backward. "Maybe. Maybe not. Now, I have things to tend to in the kitchen. Luncheon will be served at two sharp in the dining room."

"Two?" Maxine gawked. "Why, I'll starve to death by then."

Dismissing her mother with an "if only" glare, Brandy turned wary eyes on Boomer. "Everything go okay while I was gone?"

A smile bloomed ever-so slowly on his handsome face. Glancing at a blushing Natalie, he replied, "Everything's fine now, boss. Just fine." Pausing, he added, "Oh, except Roxanne."

"Roxanne? What's happened to Roxanne?"

"She's handed in her resignation."

All the stress of the past weeks knotted tightly in her temple. Raising a hand to massage her forehead, she asked skeptically, "Why?"

"Said she got a better job offer somewhere else. More money."

"More money," she groaned. "I was planning a pay raise soon."

"Really?" Boomer's dark eyes lightened a shade or two.

"For the maids," she reiterated. "Maria and Roxanne were hired in at too low a rate." She went to the file cabinet, pulled out a stack of applications. "Guess I'll be helping Maria again until someone's hired."

"I could do that for you," Boomer offered, reaching for the documents and easily retrieving them from her. "I'll look them over, call in a few apps for you to interview."

"You sure?" she asked guiltily.

"You bet." And he gave her his winning smile.

"Thanks, Boomer. Maybe you do deserve a raise after all." With a sigh, and a we'll-talk-later look at her sister, Brandy escaped to the kitchen to begin plans for Christmas dinner at the close of the week.

Maxine's eyes followed Brandy. "Humph! Just as haughty as ever," she mumbled, raising her nose and crossing the gleaming hardwood floors to ascend the stairs. Sure, her room was cramped, but it was much more preferable to the chilly reception she'd just received from her snobby daughter!

She'd managed to avoid Maxine the past few days. Though Christmas was fast approaching, and evading her for the holidays was something even Brandy wouldn't do, it was a comfort knowing she'd been spared thus far. She'd put in her time, entertain her mother as she would any guest—and pray for the swift passage of time.

Swinging the Land Rover out of the driveway and onto the blacktop, Brandy concentrated on the meeting with Soloman, only minutes away. She'd accepted that adopting Kyle was a bit on the extreme side, given the fact that his uncle was truly passionate about becoming his father. Reluctantly, she admitted that he was a good father, a loving, caring replacement for Kyle's sudden orphaned state. But that didn't mean that she couldn't fight for partial custody rights, or at the very least, visitation.

Accelerating, she headed toward Mystic. Her heart ached to see Kyle again, to hold him, to watch him grow. But melded in there somewhere, she silently admitted, she also longed for Dante's touch, for his arms about her...for his love.

But that would never happen. He was determined to keep Kyle to himself, and he'd made his stance very clear.

He didn't trust her.

And maybe she didn't trust herself.

Only a minute beyond the inn, a movement caught her eye. Her foot pressed the brake, slowed her to a creep. Across the roadside ditch and over the pasture fence to her right, she saw a dark head bobbing along. The trench, cut for weather drainage, sliced upward toward the fence where the field leveled off well above the lane. As she crept along, her eyes strained to catch a glimpse of the figure again.

She was nearing the old groundskeeper's house. Nearly a hundred years before, it'd been a part of the same tract of land that the inn sat on. As the story went, during the Depression the owners had been forced to let the groundskeeper go and sell off the cottage along with ten acres. It was a prime piece of land, fertile with rolling hills, the small recently remodeled bungalow nestled quaintly at the foreground. When Ian had bought the inn, he'd made an offer on the land next door, only to be rejected by the elderly couple who now resided there. According to the real estate agent, they had had no intention of ever selling.

As she approached the asphalt driveway of the cottage, the head gained a body.

Kyle!

There, perched happily upon Dante's shoulder, was little Kyle, bundled against the icy wind like a pig in a blanket.

Her tires screeched. She pressed the electrical window button. "What in the hell are you doing all the way out here?" she asked incredulously through the open window, the nippy air sucking the warmth right out of the vehicle.

Dante stopped, turned, and sauntered toward the fence.

"Bran-ma!" Kyle bounced gleefully upon his uncle's shoulders.

"Hush, Kyle," Dante scowled, placing his gloved hand upon the wooden post. "We were taking a walk."

"It's a long walk from Chicago to here," she pointed out. Her eyes were starving for them, soaking up the picture he made, all rugged in a worn coat and jeans, the child ironically softening the rough edges.

"I didn't walk from Chicago," he turned and began strolling along the fence row, his eyes focused stubbornly ahead of him.

She accelerated gently, following along beside him. "What—what are you doing walking out in the field by my house?"

His hands gripped Kyle's legs as he sped up the pace. "Kyle was antsy. Thought I'd take him for a walk."

Her eyes fell upon the "For Sale" sign planted in the yard of the bungalow. When had it been placed on the market? Then, just as her gaze went to slice back to the man and child, she saw it. Placed boldly above the real estate logo was one simple, bright red word: "Sold."

A mixture of glee and anger simmered, then came to a rolling boil within her. "You bought the house next door?"

Swinging Kyle off his shoulders, he carefully set him over the fence and into the cottage yard. Gripping the wooden post, Dante hurdled his massive body over the white-washed wooden fence slats and landed next to Kyle.

"Yes." Ignoring her, he swept the child up into his arms and marched toward the narrow covered porch.

She was momentarily stunned, unsure what to do. But a moment was all it took for her to shove the gearshift into first and squeal into his driveway. The door flew open and she dropped from the high seat, then slammed the door with all her might.

"You sonofabitch!" she growled, following dangerously on his tail.

He whirled on her like a hurricane of torrential force. "Shut up! Don't talk that way with Kyle near," he warned, his teeth grinding tightly together.

She could barely breathe, such was the depth of her emotions. Kyle squirmed and shimmied down Dante's front until his little boots hit the ground. His azure eyes rose to soothe her with his innocence, and he threw his arms around her legs, squeezing with such strength, she was forced to free herself and kneel before him.

"Hi, sweetie," she said breathlessly, her hands exploring his chubby cheeks, his arms, all thick within the confines of his winter wrap. "I've missed you."

"Miss you, Bran-ma," he said softly, then stepped forward and wrapped his arms around her neck.

Brandy didn't waste a moment. With a relieved, blissful sigh, she welcomed him into her embrace, relishing the warmth of him, the softness, the scent of innocence. Her eyes rose to clash with Dante's. She watched as he shoved a gloved hand through his long black hair, shifted from foot to foot.

He was worried, she decided. He was afraid Kyle would become attached to her and complicate the whole court case. Well, so be it. Court case or not, she would never stop seeking out the love of this child.

"Brandy..." his voice trailed off in warning.

She merely raised a responsive brow.

"Don't."

Her arms tightened around the tiny bundle. "I love him. You can't tell me 'don't.'"

Uninterested now in the intense adult conversation, Kyle wiggled free and toddled off to the tire swing that hung from a grand oak tree at the corner of the house.

"Why didn't you tell me?" she demanded, standing now to plant her hands on her hips.

He warily studied the green shards of ire in her eyes. She was beautiful, he accepted, not for the first time. But beauty did not necessarily make for a good mother. "Am I required to report to you every move I make?"

Her small nostrils flared. She could smell the unmistakable manly scent of him, and it angered her further. "How long have you been here?"

He shrugged and stuffed his hands in his coat pocket. "A couple days."

"That's two days I could have been seeing him," she pointed out, her boots crunching on the sparse snow that remained upon the dead yellow grass. "You really *don't* trust me, do you?"

He inhaled, sighed heavily. "Look, Brandy, I may be a lawyer myself, but in this case, I've hired my partner to represent me. And it's his legal advice that Kyle not see you until…unless the case goes halfway your way."

Splinters of fear and confusion perforated her gut. What if it *didn't* go her way—even halfway? She turned momentarily and her gaze wondered to the angelic child. What would she do without those little arms around her, that husky diminutive voice calling her Bran-ma, the scent of him around her?

"Then why did you torment me by buying the house next door?" she turned back and whispered, fighting to hold back the tears. "How can this possibly help your case?"

Flexing his fists within his pockets, he longed to reach for her, to soothe her, to make this whole damn mess of Ian's evaporate into the icy air. *Damn you to hell, Ian*, he thought yet again.

"Kyle's been missing Julie. I want him to be near her, to be able to see her every day."

"And you want to keep an eye on his inheritance," she accused, the lump in her throat clutching painfully to her voice box. "Don't trust me in business either, huh, Dante?"

His eyes slid over her shoulder to fall upon Kyle as he struggled to climb into the swing. "He's Ian's son."

"Don't remind me," she spat, venom oozing from her every pore.

"Look, Brandy," he tried again to explain his sudden decision to rearrange his life—*their* lives, he reluctantly admitted. "Whether you want to accept it or not, Kyle will inherit half of Ian's estate when he comes of age. I'm sorry you had to be caught in the middle of Ian's selfish lifestyle, but Kyle is a total innocent in this. I'll never do anything unless it's for his sake…even if it's going to hurt…someone else."

"Can I see him, spend time with him, then?" her eyes sparkled with hope as she pressed a hand to his chest.

The muscle over his jaw twitched. "No."

She snatched her hand back as if bitten. "Why are you doing this to me?"

"My lawyer—"

"Fuck your lawyer!"

Though she hissed it low enough for Kyle to be none the wiser, his eyes shifted warily to the child, then back to her. "I think you better go."

"Dante," came a feminine voice from the screen door of the cottage. "Dante, is that you?"

Brandy's gaze sliced to the familiar voice. Roxanne Perkins, her maid who'd just quite days ago, was poking her head out the front door. Oh, but of course.

"Well, hello, Roxanne," Brandy sauntered forward to stand at the bottom of the few steps that ascended to the front porch. "Have you found a new job yet?"

Roxanne, her bleach-blonde long hair hanging loose, slowly stepped out onto the porch. Her arresting blue eyes shifted guiltily to her ex-boss. "Yes."

"Really?" Brandy set a booted foot upon the bottom stair. "And where would that be?"

Dante chose that moment to interject. "I hired her," he said blandly, hating himself at that moment, even more than he did Ian. Lowering his fatigued body to the steps, he propped his elbows behind him.

Eyes averted from her, he continued flatly, "You'll be glad to know that Kyle doesn't have to go to day care anymore."

She stared down at him for an eternity, wounds of anger and pain ripping through her heart. Instead of allowing Kyle's stepmother who loved him, who *ached* to be with, to care for him daily, he'd hired *her* maid away from her for the job!

She couldn't stop the tears that'd been threatening to fall for the last few minutes. Swiping them from her cheeks, she spun on her heel and marched to her waiting vehicle. As she prepared to back from the cottage driveway, she only had eyes for the little child who stood with one leg stuck in the tire swing while he waved frantically at her. She threw the vehicle in reverse and sped away.

CHAPTER 13

"Interesting," Soloman steepled his hands, peering at her over the tips of his fingers. "For a man hell-bent on keeping you from the child, it's odd that he should buy the house next door."

"There's nothing odd about it," Brandy shifted impatiently in her chair, stilled agitated, having come straight to Sol's office after the scene with Dante. "He did it to torment me. Oh, he says it's so Kyle can be near Julie's grave, but I'm telling you, he's cruelly dangling the child just out of my reach, and all the while he's got his eye on *my* property. He's a vulture, plain and simple, and if I'd have known that before..."

Soloman was an astute lawyer, an expert at dissecting words and their underlying meaning. "Before you slept with him?"

"No!" She saw the bland look of mistrust in his beady eyes. "Yes."

"Any chance you could be pregnant?" his brows jiggled with hope.

Her hand came to rest upon her flat belly. "No," she glared at him, hating the way he always seemed to pry like some busybody old maid. "I'm infertile."

"Darn," he snapped his fingers. "Well, that leaves us to proceed as planned. The visitation and custody hearing are set for January twentieth. I want you to come dressed conservatively, as little skin as possible showing. Judge Walker is extremely right wing. And wear your hair down. You don't want to look too prim or—"

"Sol."

"What?"

"I get the picture."

No, she didn't get the picture, he thought anxiously. She didn't know just how badly he wanted to best Dante Saxon. And she didn't realize how very sexy she was, how extremely difficult it would be to downplay those pouty lips and smoldering eyes so that she'd appear more matronly, and therefore, motherly to the judge.

"Well, then," he pushed himself from his desk and stood. "Between now and then, if you have any questions, concerns, don't hesitate to call or stop in."

Brandy peeled herself from the comfortable chair and began donning her coat. "All the questions I have, Sol," she shoved her hands into ski gloves, "only God can answer."

Days later, Christmas Eve finally arrived. The inn was decorated with holly and mistletoe, strings of multicolored twinkling lights, and a massive fir tree proudly occupied the recreation room indoors. Bright foil-wrapped gifts filled the base of the tree, Christmas carols played softly on the downstairs speaker system and the scents of eggnog and glazed ham and peppermint wafted the air. A fire crackled in the hearth and a young couple celebrating their first anniversary, the only guests at the inn for the holidays, sat cozied up on the love seat before the fire.

"Meez MacKay?" Pedro, a small man with dark eyes and skin, and salt-and-pepper hair, scampered into the rec room where Brandy was wiping down bar tables. "Maria and me, we go now, sí?"

It'd been over a week since she'd left Chicago, just days since her tension-filled encounter with Dante next door, and her mind just wasn't focusing. She could only feel the constant pain in her heart of being without little Kyle, and he was only next door! The shame of Dante's mistrust in her, Dante's overall rejection after their phenomenal lovemaking and the scene at the bungalow were all taking their toll on her.

Now, Maxine had come to dredge the whole past back up, like exhuming a dead body, Brian's little body, to be exact. Her presence, that scornful look, was all it took for Brandy to relive the panic, the pain, the anguish of her neglect of her little brother. And Dante sure hadn't helped in that respect, either.

As she scrubbed the table top, plucking up the empty beer bottle, an image of Brian came vividly to her. Blonde, blue-eyed, and as mischievous as Kyle, he'd been the love of her life. She hadn't minded baby sitting him every day after school. In fact, she'd looked forward to it, to their romps together in the crunchy leaves, carrying him piggyback as he squealed with delight, long strolls up the sidewalk of their quiet suburban Chicago neighborhood, a safe community—until that day over fifteen years ago.

"Meez MacKay?" Pedro tried again, placing a small hand on her shoulder.

Brandy jerked, the bottle in her hand clanging against the edge of the table. "Oh! Pedro," she placed a hand to her chest. "You startled me."

"*Por favor*, please forgive me," he snatched his hand back, fearful of further upsetting his boss. She'd been very distracted since returning from Chicago this last trip, and he and Maria were concerned that their employment would be threatened. He was well aware the budget had been getting tighter and tighter of late.

Brandy shook her head and climbed up onto a high bar stool. "Oh, Pedro," she replied, folding her arms and placing them on the table. With a sigh, her head fell to rest comfortably in the crook of her arm. "I'm sorry. I've just been so stressed lately."

"And sad, *mi petite*?" Pedro had a knack for communication, despite the language barrier. In fact, he could rival her own sister.

"Yes, Pedro," Brandy agreed softly, raising her head. "And sad. But don't concern yourself with that. You and Maria run along. As long as the Christmas menu is planned and ready for tomorrow, you're free to go."

"But we come back, no?" he asked, his silver eyebrows dipping to complete a frown.

Brandy smiled gently, placing a hand at Pedro's elbow. "Oh, but of course you'll come back. I need you and Maria. Now I know the finances are getting tight, but as long as the inn is open, you have a job." She slid from the seat and embraced her prized chef, a man who'd taught her much about the art of cooking. "But don't come back until after Christmas. Take a few paid days off."

Pedro's relieved smile was accompanied by a nervous laugh. "*Sí, sí,*" he nodded, backing from the recreation room. "*Feliz Navidad,* Meez MacKay!"

"Merry Christmas, Pedro," Brandy murmured, suddenly alone in the room.

Yeah, it was going to be some merry Christmas, she groaned inwardly.

"There you are!" Natalie chimed, entering the room with Boomer and his daughter, Rachelle.

Brandy carried a large gray basin to the bar, then loaded it with several dishes that had been left behind by her guests, the young couple who'd just stolen away to their room as she'd been in conversation with Pedro. "Yep, here I am," she murmured sarcastically. *All alone.*

"Hi, Brandy!" Rachelle said in a bubbly tone, claiming a bar table. A teenager, Rachelle was delighted to mingle with the adults. Tall and built solidly like her father, she was a striking young woman with black hair, pale almond skin, and extraordinary cocoa eyes. "Let's all have a drink," she coaxed.

Boomer slid into the chair next to his daughter. "Think again, Ray," he called her by her pet name. "Tea or soda pop for you, kiddo."

"I know," she chided her dad, winking at him. "Just testin' ya."

Natalie giggled softly, delighted at this young girl who'd been a source of entertainment since Boomer had taken her home to meet Rachelle. "And he's not budging," she offered, spying the forlorn look on her sister's face. In seconds, she was behind the bar, cornering her. "Are you okay, honey?"

"Yes, fine."

"Come join us for some pre-Christmas cheer. You need a break."

"No," Brandy tossed the dish rag into the sink. "I need Max to get the hell out of here. If she stays much longer, I'm going AWOL."

"She's only staying a few more days," Natalie led Brandy to a seat next to Rachelle. "Now you sit here, and I'll be the waitress for everyone."

Natalie reached for a round cork tray and notepad, loving the idea of playing waitress after years of examining hundreds of people's demented minds. "Now," she replied huskily, her blue eyes soaking Boomer with a look that only lovers would be able to decipher. "What for the gorgeous giant?"

Boomer roared deeply, his gaze penetrating hers. "Beer. Just a beer."

"Oh, gawd," Rachelle simulated sticking her finger down her throat. "You two are gross."

Brandy was jolted from her dreary world. "You two...?" she asked in awe, her eyes bouncing from Boomer to Natalie.

Boomer shifted uncomfortably in his seat, nearly toppling it over. "Rachelle, darling, did I ever tell you that you have a very big mouth?"

"Why thank you, Daddy, dear," she purred, displaying a large set of pearly white teeth. "Now, I'll have a Coke, Natalie, and some of those stick pretzels."

Natalie nodded, jotting down the orders on her pad. Glancing up expectantly at her sister, she asked, "And you, Brandy?"

Brandy blew out a breath and smiled weakly. "You two. I never would have guessed that, the way you were at each other's throats that day I went to see…"

Natalie was an astute therapist. Instantly, she patted Brandy's hand. "It was something you had to do. Now, I'll bring you a daiquiri, say, hmm, strawberry?"

Brandy shrugged. "Sure."

When Natalie went to work on their orders, Brandy asked Boomer, "Did you transfer the lines to the cell phone?"

Boomer unclipped the phone from his belt loop and slid it across the table. "Check."

"Did you pay the utilities?"

Boomer's eyes shifted. "Uncheck," he made a face. "I was waiting to make this next deposit. If I don't wait, the money won't be there."

Brandy sighed audibly. The bills had been piling up, and she was a month behind in the mortgage. But she refused to raise her rates. Help. She desperately needed financial help. That was all there was to it. And if Dante didn't offer to assist with half the expenses soon—because he was, after all, the present guardian of the other half-owner, Kyle—she would have to resort to another form of litigation against him. It was all too clear to her now, that court was the only alternative to communication with him.

Boomer grasped her hand, squeezing encouragingly. "We'll make it, Brandy. Don't you worry. You can never expect huge profits when you first start a new business." And he knew first hand. He'd attempted to open his own gym before packing Rachelle up for a new start. It had failed, but not because he couldn't keep up with the bills—though that had been a struggle. Laura had owed thousands to her dealer. Boomer had sold his gym after Laura had passed away, and had paid her debts off in cash, leaving himself and Rachelle with just enough to relocate to Wisconsin.

"Now, now," Natalie purred, placing a frothy pink drink in front of Brandy. "Keep your hands off my sister," she warned, sending a wink across the table to Boomer.

He released Brandy's hand and drawled, "When the cat's away…"

"I'm gonna go play a video game," Rachelle mumbled, disgusted with adult innuendo. With that, she took her Coke and pretzels to the crowded corner where the games were set up.

"Cat?" came the voice that Brandy had been dreading all day. "There's a cat in here?" Maxine was appalled, crossing the room to take a seat at the round table to Brandy's right.

"No, no, Mother," Natalie completed serving the drinks. "Never mind. Would you like a drink?"

Looking down her slim nose at the enormous cocktail that Brandy clutched, she snarled, "I don't drink, and you know it. Now, I'll have a Perrier with a slice of lemon."

Natalie responded with silence, sending Brandy a look that said, 'don't bite.' She went to do her mother's bidding.

"You used to drink," Brandy accused, toying with her straw, then taking a long sip.

A lengthy silence cracked the air. Maxine's brows lifted, and she sent Brandy a chilly look. "Only before Brian was taken."

The room was deathly still, then Rachelle stepped back over, still keeping her ears perked, and asked. "Who's Brian?"

Brandy sucked the slush off the end of her straw, gripped the fish-bowl-sized cocktail glass, then spun in her chair until her back was nearly parallel to Maxine's sour face. "He was my little brother."

"Was?" Rachelle's interest was peaked.

"Rachelle!" Boomer shifted uncomfortably in his seat. "It's none of your business."

Rachelle poked a defiant tongue out at her dad.

"It's okay, honey," Brandy tossed the straw aside and tipped the drink back, grateful that Natalie had mixed it strong. "I'll tell you before Maxine has a chance. I was baby sitting him—I was only thirteen. We were out in the front yard. The phone rang." Brandy locked her teeth tightly together. "I decided to run in and answer it."

"And leave my precious boy *alone!*" Maxine hissed, her eyes spewing like lava.

"Mother!" Natalie scolded, having just returned to the table to overhear the conversation.

"What?" Maxine turned in her seat to pin her other daughter with a pained glare. "It's the truth. She left my baby alone, and someone snatched him up." Wagging a slim, decorated finger at Brandy, she spat, "And it's all her fault that I'll never see him again!"

Brandy shoved her drink across the table, then slid out of her seat. "I have lots of work to do."

"Brandy," Natalie slammed the Perrier bottle on the table, startling Maxine. Placing a gentling hand on Brandy's arm, she said in a hushed tone, "Don't go. Face her for once. You can't keep running. You need to finally have it out with her."

Brandy had been staring straight ahead, but at her sister's words, she turned tear-filled, sparkling green eyes on Natalie. "Always the therapist, aren't you, Doctor?"

"Let her go," Maxine sneered. "She'll never stop running. Never take responsibility for anything, and especially not for Brian." She smirked. "And here she is trying to get custody of poor Ian's child…"

"Yes," Brandy mumbled as she turned to leave. "Poor Ian."

"I think she's a very good person."

The voice had come from the corridor. The tension crackled in the air as all eyes turned to the source.

Boomer shot to his feet, sending the barstool crashing to the floor. Like lightning, he shot across the room and came to stand before Dante. "What are you doing here?" he demanded.

"I'm here to see Brandy," Dante's glare slid over Boomer, assessing the bulk of him. True, he was a giant, but no one was going to stop him with a baby in his arms.

"Oh, no you're not," Boomer crossed thick arms over an even thicker chest and planted his bulk in the doorway. "You've already done enough to her. Now hit the road."

"Boomer!" Brandy suddenly gasped, having gotten over the shock of seeing Dante standing in the hallway, all tall and alarmingly handsome, effortlessly balancing a sleeping Kyle in one arm.

Boomer turned only his head, his feet remaining planted. "What? You mean you *want* to see this joker? Brandy, man, he's only gonna break your heart—again."

"Who in the hell is that man?" Maxine demanded, marching over to stand at Boomer's side.

"That's enough! All of you just go back to your little party," Brandy crossed the room, dodging tables, then wedged herself between Dante, and Boomer and Maxine. Her back to Dante, she tilted her head back to address Boomer. "Boomer. Please."

Boomer's dark eyes narrowed as he shot Dante a heated look over Brandy's head. "Brandy, man…" he began, shaking his head. Glancing down at his boss, he saw the pleading look in her eyes. Blowing out a resigned breath he said, "I'll be right here if you need me."

Maxine snorted. "Brandy, you certainly don't deserve all this attention. Now I demand to know what's going on here."

Dante's eyes singed Maxine. "Frankly, ma'am, it's none of your business."

"Well!" Maxine sucked in a breath, stomping one foot as she crossed her arms. "Just who do you think you are, anyway?" she demanded, then turned gleaming eyes on her daughter. "Brandy, are you going to let this insolent man talk to your mother like that?"

"Yes, I am," she replied softly, stuffing her hands into her pants pockets.

Maxine wagged a finger at her daughter. "You always were such a little snot!"

"Ms.—er, Hart, is it?" Dante put a protective hand against Kyle's head. "Do you mind? You're going to wake him."

Before Maxine could respond, Brandy guided Dante down the hallway, around the stairs, and into the living room. "I'm sorry for my mother. She's a very demanding, nosy person."

Dante allowed her to steer him to the sofa. He lowered himself gently, bracing Kyle for the shift in position. "And seems to hold a grudge against you."

She went to the tree, bent and picked up a flat, square gift wrapped in bright green. "Yes. But enough of her. Here," she crossed and extended it toward him as he settled into the cushions. "I got you a Christmas gift."

He looked blankly at it before slowly reaching out for it. "You didn't have to do that."

"No," she pressed it into his hand. "I didn't, but I wanted to. It's really nothing. Go ahead and open it."

"Now?"

She smiled softly. "Yes, now."

He hesitated only a moment before tearing into it, mindful of waking Kyle. When the item was revealed, his expression transformed from excited to stunned. "I—I'm speechless. How did you get it?"

It was a photograph of Julie and Kyle framed by a rich maple filagreed wood.

She watched, touched, as he lightly ran a fingertip over the surface. "Mr. Goldberg, a guest that was here just before Julie passed away, took it. He's a photographer."

His eyes caressed the classic freeze-frame of beautiful mother cuddling handsome son. It was a gift from the heart, and his eyes rose to meet hers. "Thank you. I don't think I've ever gotten a more meaningful present."

She took a seat across from him, warmed by the faint tears in his eyes. "You're welcome. Now, I would love to know why you're here."

Shaking his head to clear the sentiment, he replied. "Well, against my partner's advice, I've come to let Kyle stay for a day or two."

Brandy gasped, her eyes gleaming with tears of joy. "You mean it?"

Dante saw the pure delight in her eyes, and at that moment, he became certain he'd made the right decision in coming here. "I'm still going through with the case. Kyle needs a legal guardian established for a number of reasons. But he's been…"

The excitement, the gratitude she felt at that moment, was overwhelming, pure bliss. Without attempting to hide her smile, she prompted, "Been what?"

Dante searched her face, saw there the beautiful woman that he'd become enamored with long ago, when he'd seen Ian's picture of his wife. Somehow, he'd allowed himself to be drawn to her, even seduced her during that sacred mourning period. And yet, he held his nephew's future in his hands. How had he allowed the inevitable, Julie's death and subsequently, his ready-made fatherhood, to become entangled with a beguiling woman's plight of widowhood? Looking at her now, her shimmering hair glowing about her shoulders like an angel's cloak of gold, her eyes like soft spring grass, he wondered how he was going to disentangle her from his mind, his life, when he now offered her a small place in Kyle's life.

"He's been missing you—and Julie, of course," he admitted. "But I think he needs a female figure right now, to buffer the loss of his mother. Could you handle him and the inn at the same time?"

"Oh, could I ever!" she breathed, rising, only to drop to her knees before him. Placing a feather-light hand over Kyle's warm back, she added, "I have Boomer, and all the other staff, as well as Natalie. She took a month off, but she's staying one more week."

Dante sighed with relief. "Good. I just don't want him left alone."

Brandy's eyes rose to his, transforming from sparkling, to steaming green. "It won't happen again. I was only thirteen when Brian disappeared. If you haven't already noticed, I'm an adult now."

Lord, how he'd noticed she *was* an adult, a very gorgeous, caring, responsible woman. Maxine Hart's hateful words about her own daughter came to mind, and he found himself silently defending

Brandy—and feeling a stab of guilt for implying that he too, didn't
trust her. "I—I didn't mean to suggest..."

"Of course you didn't," she snarled softly. She would never be able
to rid herself of that stigma, but she was going to prove to him that
she was capable, despite being unable to change the horrible past.
Setting her jaw firm, she then asked, "And what of Roxanne?"

He shifted uncomfortably, glanced across the room. "I let her go."

"Let her go."

"Yes. Her heart..." he finally swung his gaze back to hers, "wasn't
with Kyle. She had other things in mind."

"I see," Brandy wasn't surprised, well aware that Roxanne had
always looked out for number one. "Well," she combed a hand
through the soft dark curls at Kyle's chubby neck. "I guess second-
best is better than not at all."

"Look, I'll be up front with you," Dante blew out a breath, reached
a hand up to cover hers at Kyle's back. Lord, how tiny and soft her
hand was! "I have loads of work hanging over my head. Roxanne was
dismissed yesterday, and that left me high and dry. I don't want to
deposit him in a daycare in Mystic—at least not yet—so I have no
choice but to come and beg you to take him for a couple days." *And
Martin will hopefully never hear of it*, he thought with a mental sigh.

"Oh," she stood, wrenching her hand from his hot one, and
hugged herself. It was suddenly chilly in the room. "So I'm only a
temporary solution."

He stood slowly, like a practiced father able to juggle a sleeping
son. "Look at it how you want, Brandy," he said evenly, almost
blandly. "But the fact is, Kyle needs you, and so do I."

They needed her! she thought gleefully. If only it were true—and
permanent!

She thought of Brian, looked intently at Kyle, her arms aching to
hold him.

No, she couldn't bring Brian back. But these next few days, she'd
damn well prove to be the best substitute for Julie that Dante would

ever dream of. She would show him this once that it was in their best interests, foremost, Kyle's, for them to all be together.

And this may very well be her only chance to prove it.

Kyle needed a family, a mother *and* a father. But Dante would most likely never see it that way, and she was only hurting herself further by continuing to think that someday he would. She would take this one chance to prove it, but it would be her last. If he continued to mistrust her, she needed to move on, to put Kyle and Dante behind her, to give up the custody suit. That was precisely why she'd just silently made the decision to sell out her half of the inn to Dante, something that'd been crossing her mind recently. For love, she would sacrifice her dream of owning her own bed and breakfast. And for love, she'd walk out of his life forever.

Gently pulling Kyle from his arms and tucking him into her own, she whispered, "Thank you, Dante. This is the best Christmas present ever."

Days later, there was a line of guests from the office window, curling out into the foyer. Most were new arrivals, waiting to check into their reserved suites, while the ones waiting to check out were the lovebirds who'd compromised her system by sleeping in too late. Now, some of her arriving guests would be forced to wait in the bar, and she would be obliged to comp them with free drinks and hors d'oeuvres to pacify them while their suite was being cleaned.

Natalie was in the kitchen assisting Pedro with the upcoming evening meal preparations, and she'd allowed Boomer to take the day off to take Rachelle to the doctor, but how was she supposed to have foreseen this chaos?

"Kyle!" she reached for him, while simultaneously sliding Robert Frank's credit card through the machine. "Sorry." She blew out a breath, handing him back his card, then plucking Kyle off a nearby copy machine. "He's a real handful."

"Quite all right." Robert, a retired stunt man from Hollywood, was passing through with his wife on their way to Maine for a family reunion. "I don't blame the boy. There's an addictive thrill in teetering on the edge of danger," he replied, clicking his tongue and pretending to snip Kyle's nose between his fingers.

Kyle began to whine, pulling away from the large man on the other side of the counter, checking his face for the nose that he was sure was being held between the stranger's bent finger joints.

"It's okay, sweetie," Brandy chuckled softly, hiking Kyle up further on her hip. "He's just teasing you."

When he continued to squirm, Brandy set him on the floor by the desk. "Thanks for staying with us, Mr. Frank. Next time, maybe you could—"

Robert, a man in his mid sixties, and a bit thick around the waist, suddenly began clutching at his chest, his eyes glazing over with a faraway look.

"Mr. Frank? Are you all right?"

"I—I can't breathe," he panted, his body slowly slipping lower as he struggled to hold onto the counter with one shaky hand.

Brandy reached across for him just as he fell back against the next guest in line. "Mr. Frank!"

She then heard a sickening thud. Racing from the office, the door flying widely ajar, she went to her guest and knelt at his side where he'd landed on his back in the entryway. He was rapidly taking on a pallid skin tone, and gasping heavily for air. Everyone's eyes were on him, but no one moved, all guests frozen in shock.

"Mrs. White," she glanced quickly up at the middle-aged writer who'd returned to rebook her stay. "Pick up the office phone and dial nine-one-one!" she demanded. "Now!"

Mary White always panicked in a crisis. It was precisely why she preferred *writing* about chaos, rather than living it. "M-me?" she queried, bumping into the next guest as she backed away.

"Yes!" Brandy ordered, "just do it, *please!*" She began shaking the now unconscious Mr. Frank, calling out his name, desperately trying to remember the steps to her basic life support training she'd taken before opening the inn, precisely for an emergency such as this.

Mary snapped to attention at the innkeepers tone, going directly to dial the phone as ordered.

Leaning to look, listen, and feel for Mr. Frank's breathing, Brandy called out, "Does anyone else know CPR?" He wasn't breathing! Positioning his head, she closed off his nose and placed her mouth over his, giving him two breaths. She then felt for a pulse. There was none.

Her heart thudding against her breastbone, Brandy placed the heels of her hands over Robert's chest and began pumping.

No one came to her aid.

"One one-thousand, two one-thousand..." she counted the chest compressions. "Quick! Someone run to the kitchen and get my sister, Natalie. *Now!*"

As a patron at the rear of the line scurried to do her innkeeper's bidding, Mrs. Frank came down the stairs, her tiny frame pausing at the landing midway down. Seeing her husband spread out on the hard floor, with Brandy pumping his chest, she wailed, "Bobby! *Bobby!* What's going on? Oh, my God, Bobby!" Stumbling down the remaining stairs, Lilly Frank pushed aside the group that had gathered to gawk, and collapsed at her husband's side in tears.

"Brandy, what—?" Natalie's answer came in the form of her sister performing life saving measures on a man who was as gray as the clouds outside. Without waiting for a response, she pushed an exhausted Brandy aside and took over the chest compressions. "Do the rescue breaths, Brandy," she ordered.

Brandy obeyed, sliding into the mode with her sister as they synchronized their efforts. It was with extreme relief that Brandy heard the screaming sirens.

Just as the emergency crew burst through the front door, Robert began breathing on his own. He had a pulse, but had yet to regain consciousness. A flurry of activity began as the trained medical personnel placed a mask of oxygen on their patient, then determined his heart rhythm by a portable EKG monitor. They then started an intravenous line and assessed his vital signs.

"Is he going to be all right?" Brandy asked, completely exhausted.

The ambulance attendee shook his head and gave her a rewarding smile. "I have no way of knowing his prognosis, but you've certainly increased his odds for a second chance at life. Good job."

Lilly Frank began to sob anew. Flinging herself into Brandy's arms, she whispered, "Thank you. Thank you!"

Brandy sighed, returning the embrace. If it hadn't been so busy with all the guests lined up and Kyle being so—

"Oh my God!" Brandy gasped, flinging Lilly from her. "Kyle! Kyle, honey, where are you?"

Everyone glanced around, confused by yet another sudden crisis.

"Kyle's not with you?" Natalie asked, incredulously.

"He was right here, only minutes ago." *One minute was all it took!* she silently screamed at herself as she flew through the open office door, her eyes bouncing frantically from one corner to the next. "*Kyle!*"

There was no answer. No mischievous Kyle teetering on the edge of disaster. The office was empty.

CHAPTER 14

Racing up the hallway, Brandy flew into the kitchen. "Pedro! Have you seen Kyle? Have you?" she demanded.

"No, *senora*," he replied, somewhat taken aback at his boss' sharp tone. It was his first day back from the nice vacation she'd given him, and he prayed she wasn't upset with him. The butcher's knife paused over a huge head of lettuce, he added, "Maybe my Maria see little Kyle, no?"

Brandy felt her head twirling. It was all happening again. Just as with Brian, Kyle had been there one moment, and...gone the next. *God in heaven, please,* she prayed, spinning on her heel and dashing down the hallway and up the stairs. *Please let me find him!*

"Have you found him yet?" Natalie called up the stairs.

"No!" she screamed, taking the steps two at a time.

"I'll check downstairs," Natalie shouted, hastening her steps toward the dining and living area.

Brandy entered each suite one at a time, flinging the doors back, some standing ajar as the maid performed her duties from room to room, double checking rooms that had been cleaned days ago and closed off for future guests. Maria paused as she flipped a quilt over the bed where the lovely couple had made love.

"Have you seen Kyle?" Brandy screeched, her breathing coming heavily.

"No, *senora*," Maria's midnight eyes formed startled round pools. "Not for hours."

Brandy didn't stay to offer an explanation. Whirling, she went on to the next suite. "*Kyle!*" she shouted, entering the room, slinging back the curtains to reveal a private balcony, complete with a steaming hot tub. Oh, Lord, no! she begged, stepping closer to the tub. Her heart pounding, she flipped on the underwater light.

Thank you, God, she breathed, when she saw that there was no tiny body floating in the hot tub.

Glancing frantically about, she had nearly spun around to exit the balcony, when a small dark spot beyond the patch of firs and elms behind the inn caught her eye. Despite the recent partial thaw, the thick lake ice had persisted, but there, on the edge, Brandy saw a hole in the ice. Kyle? Was that teeny speck on the water, Kyle's dark head?

Fighting a wave of dizziness, Brandy flew from the room and down the stairs.

"What is it!" Natalie demanded, seeing the pale expression on her sister's face.

Brandy swallowed hard, leaping down the stairs. "I think I see him in the lake!" she threw over her shoulder, racing to the rear entrance.

Brandy didn't bother with a coat or boots. She flew out the rear door, crossed the balcony, and vaulted into the slushy snow.

Footprints. There were tiny little footprints in the mushy snow. *And they led to the lake!*

Dante burst through the double doors to the Pediatric Intensive Care Unit where Kyle had been transported by helicopter to Chicago Regional. He didn't take time to ask directions to where he could find his nephew. It only took seconds for him to hear her sobs.

Racing across the gleaming waxed floor, he flung back the curtain. "Kyle!" he breathed, tears coming to his eyes as he took in the scene before him. In a cold metal crib, he lay with an oxygen mask swallowing his little face, while his arms were held captive on each side by arm boards supporting intravenous lines. He was breathing, thank God, but unconscious, as if he lay safely in his own bed at home, resting in contented slumber. Monitors and IV pumps surrounded his tiny body as he lay adorned in a tiny blue hospital gown covered in Winnie the Pooh—ironically his favorite cartoon character.

Brandy was seated at the side of the crib, both arms reaching in to hold his tiny hand. Her face was pressed against the bars, as if she were a prisoner being segregated from him. At the panicked sound of Dante's voice, she glanced at him through the crib rails.

"Dante," she whispered huskily, her eyes red-rimmed as they had been that day at Ian's funeral.

Looking over the lifeless body of the child that had become his lifeline, Dante nearly growled, "How could you? How could you have taken your eyes off him for even a *second*?"

"I...I—"

He cut her off abruptly, his voice rising as his eyes turned to tears of gold. "There's no excuse!"

Brandy slowly released Kyle's limp hand, then rose to stand so that she could see Dante over the top of the crib. "I suppose you're going to use this against me in the custody case, aren't you, Dante?" she asked disbelieving, choking on her own tears. "It was an accident, something that can happen to anyone, and you're going to use this to prevent me from even getting visitation rights." She knew it with all her heart, could see the mistrust, the...hate in his eyes.

But she knew now, as she'd vowed days ago, that she'd see that the court case proceedings would be dissolved. Kyle was all his, and she'd step out of their lives for good—after she was sure Kyle was going to be okay.

Dante sighed heavily, coming closer to reach a hand in and lightly caress Kyle's cool cheek. "Never mind. Let's drop it for now."

"Drop it?" she sniffled, rounding the crib to stand where Dante had entered the small room a minute earlier.

A nurse entered the room, introducing herself. Dante went around to take the seat Brandy had just vacated. Turning his back on Brandy, he anxiously queried the nurse. "How is he? Is he going to be okay?"

The nurse reprogrammed the IV fluid rate on the pump. Adjusting the warming blanket that Kyle was tucked into, she replied, "His vital signs are stable…his core temperature is finally approaching normal. He's breathing on his own, which is a miracle in itself. Now we just wait for him to gain consciousness."

"How long was he in the water?" Dante asked, his eyes swinging over to pin Brandy with the question. But she was gone. With a mixture of relief and guilt, Dante attentively waited for a positive answer.

The nurse responded to his question. "It's not known. As much as ten minutes, we suspect—"

"*Ten* minutes?" Dante shouted. Where had she been for ten minutes? Why had he been left unattended?

That was it. Even if there'd been a shred of hope, he vowed silently, she wouldn't be getting custody…or even visitation rights, for that matter. Never.

"The extremely cold temperatures of the lake water is probably what saved him," the nurse went on, keeping the tone of emotion under control. "He was preserved, in a sense, until breathing was started."

"Breathing was started immediately? His chances of brain damage…?" he asked, dreading the answer, yet desperately needing to know.

"Yes," she pulled the stethoscope from around her neck and listened to Kyle's heart and lungs. "The young lady, the one who just left. She started CPR. If she hadn't located him and started rescue breaths so soon, he most likely wouldn't be…with us right now."

"Brandy…" his eyes wandered to the vacant area where she had been standing moments ago, her heart in her eyes.

She'd *found* him. Unlike her little brother, who'd never been located. She'd found him…and given him her breath…life. Brandy had breathed life back into his…*son*.

"Could you excuse me for a few moments?" Dante asked, slipping from the room with a longing look over his shoulder at the impish child that had become the focus of his world.

"Dante." Natalie nodded solemnly, approaching him in the hall as he exited the unit.

"Where is she?" he asked, his eyes sweeping the stark-white hall.

"I think you should probably leave her alone for now."

"I need to see her!"

"She's too fragile right now. She told me…what you said to her."

Dante raked a trembling hand through his jet-black hair. Blowing out a breath, he repeated with clamped teeth, "*I need to see her!*"

Natalie crossed her arms, leaning against the concrete wall. "Dante, she's been through hell over Brian. And now this. Do you know why she took her eyes off Kyle?"

"No." Dante placed the sole of his dress shoe on the wall behind him, using it for support. Sliding his hands into his trouser pockets, he tipped his head back against the cold concrete and stared at the ceiling. "Why?"

"Kyle was closed in the office with her where she was keeping a very close eye on him. But a guest had had a heart attack in the lobby, and she raced out to start CPR on him. In the crisis situation, she left the office door open behind her and Kyle slipped out during all the emergency activity. Somehow, he even got by the cook and made it out the back door. Meanwhile, Brandy was saving a man's life. He's alive, in the Coronary Care Unit in Platteville."

Dante paled. She'd saved a life—hell, she'd saved two. She hadn't left Kyle unattended. Her heart had simply taken over as she'd reached out to save a person's life. And then she'd found Kyle and given him life, as well.

And he'd been so cruel to her.

"Jesus, Natalie. I'm so sorry. I didn't know. It's just that Kyle…I love him so much," he mumbled, closing his eyes tightly. "Where is she?"

Natalie studied the obvious remorse in his stricken expression. She'd promised Brandy that she wouldn't tell him where she was. But what the hell? She'd made a promise to Julie as well, and Julie had been right. They were meant for each other, whether they knew it or not. Besides, it wasn't the first time she'd interfered for Brandy's own good. Not like Maxine, of course…

"She's down the hall where the phones are. Calling her lawyer to withdraw from the custody case."

Dante didn't wait for further instruction. He sprinted down the hall toward the waiting area.

"I'll go sit with Kyle!" Natalie called after him.

Brandy hung up the phone and pressed her forehead to the receiver. She'd failed again. Brian had been lost as a result of her negligence, now Kyle was clinging to life for the very same reason. Her inability to conceive a child must be God's way of keeping her from causing more disaster. It was her fate. She damn well deserved it…she was a complete failure.

The sobs came from deep within her soul. Pressing her hands to the wall on either side of the phone, she banged her head against the receiver, tears flowing freely. She'd never known such pain, such hopelessness. More than losing Ian, more than Maxine's emotional abuse over the years, it was accepting her own failure, accepting the fact that, because of her own irresponsibility—oh, and how Maxine had always been right!—she would never see her brother again, and she would never become a mother to Kyle or any other child. That was the crux of what now sent her spiraling into a pit of despair.

When the arms came around her from behind, she gasped. Turning, her eyes locked with Dante's flaming ones. "What…what are you doing?" she said in soft wonderment.

"Apologizing." He pulled her hard against the length of him. One hand went up to grip the back of her neck, drawing her damp face closer. He showered her wet face, her trembling lips, with tender kisses. "I'm so sorry, Brandy. I was a total ass."

Savoring the feel of him, the masculine scent of him, for just a moment, she pulled free of his embrace. "No," her voice was raspy with emotion. "You're right. I have no excuse. I'm just not responsible enough to care for a child. I've proven that twice now. It's no wonder I'm sterile."

Dante smiled softly, tucking a stray wisp of wheat-colored hair behind her ear. "Natalie told me what happened at the inn."

Brandy's eyes narrowed. "I can't trust anyone, not even my own sister, not even...myself."

Gathering her back into his arms, Dante sighed, kissing the top of her head as he raced his hands up and down her back. She felt so good, so right in his arms. Why had he been doing this to her for so long? "You can trust me, darling. Trust me that I won't ever talk to you that way again."

Brandy closed her eyes, savoring the hardness of him, the protectiveness that surrounded her as she pressed her cheek to his silk tie. "I withdrew from the custody case."

"I know."

She lifted her face and studied the eyes of the man she loved, but could never truly have. "She told you that too?"

"Mmm-hmm," he nearly hummed, reaching for her hand. "And I think it's the most selfless, loving thing you could ever do for Kyle." Drawing her hand to his cheek, he held it there and said huskily, "Now wipe your eyes. We need to get back to him."

Without a pause for her to do just that, Dante led her back to Kyle.

❦   ❦   ❦

They were side-by-side, both reaching into the crib just to touch him, to caress his still little body, to reassure themselves that he still existed. Dante was nearest Kyle's head, rubbing gently over his brow with the pad of his thumb.

Kyle's eyes suddenly fluttered open. "Don-tee?" he croaked.

"Kyle!" Dante inhaled swiftly. "Nurse!" he called in a booming voice.

Brandy only smiled broadly, relief flooding her every cell.

The nurse raced in. "What is it?"

"He's awake—and *talking*!" Dante replied, his voice deep and choked with emotion.

The nurse pressed her palms together. Her pale eyes rose to the ceiling in a silent prayer of gratitude. She then began a thorough assessment as Kyle slowly came to life, wiggling, kicking the warming blanket away, examining the array of neat gadgets and machines surrounding him. Exiting the room, the nurse called over her shoulder, "I'll call the intensivist."

Kyle began to whine, and looked about him in sudden alarm at the tubes attached to his arms. Suddenly coming to his knees, the tubes were easily forgotten as he gripped the crib bars and attempted to push his face between them. "Mommy!" he reached both arms out to Brandy, his face lighting up with pure love.

Dante's head whipped around, but he remained silent. It was such a sweet sound, such a sweet scene, he thought with awe. He watched as Brandy paused, glanced about nervously, then shifted her feet.

"Honey, it's Brandy, not Mommy. Remember me?" she tried to redirect Kyle, her arms itching to lunge for him.

Kyle waggled a tiny finger at her as his forehead wrinkled. "No! Mommy!" he insisted, again reaching for her through the bars. "Want Mommy!"

Does he really mean me? she wondered, hopeful, yet accepting that her childless fate was imminent.

Dante raised a hand to brush a sudden falling tear from her cheek. How could he deny Kyle what he plainly wanted more than anything else? And how could he keep Brandy from that which he knew was in her heart...Kyle and motherhood and... It was then, when he saw the hopeful expression in her haunted eyes, then when he saw the love and longing pass between woman and child, that he knew their future. Hell, now that he looked back on it, he'd known it a year ago when he became snared by grieving green eyes at Ian's funeral.

Selfishly, he hadn't wanted to further complicate his own life with a woman who'd established a life far away from his in Wisconsin, and yet he'd done precisely that by seducing her, encouraging her to forget her rake of a husband. Shamefully, he also realized that he'd used the tragedy of her little brother's disappearance as an excuse to push her away, and had caused her more pain in doing so.

"Go ahead, Mom. See if the nurse will let you hold him."

Mom. The word was like heaven to her. Dante was relenting—for now—allowing Kyle to accept her as his mother. But she couldn't do that to Kyle. "No. That's okay. You go ahead and hold him."

Dante withdrew his hand from her. "But you're his mother now. And he wants you."

Her eyes searched his, praying, hoping beyond hope. But her mind was clouded by her own uncertainties. "I appreciate what you're doing, Dante, but I don't think it's a good idea to confuse him."

Dante's dark brows rose in mock puzzlement. "Confuse him? How can it confuse him to have his own mother holding him?"

"But...but I'm not—"

"Yes, you are!" Dante hooked a hand at the back of her neck and tugged her closer, his hot lips meeting her startled ones. "And I'm his father now."

She shook her head as if to clear the cobwebs. "What—what do you mean?"

"I mean," he began, his lips slanting over hers as he sighed inwardly at the relief of what he was about to do, at how right it felt, "that we are a family. That is," he added, cupping her face with both hands before planting another kiss on her astounded mouth, "if you'll marry us."

Her lips froze. Withdrawing from him, she probed his eyes, and saw there, an immeasurable amount of emotion that he was bestowing completely on her. "Do you mind repeating that?" she croaked, her hands gripping his wrists.

"I said, will you marry us?"

"Us?"

Dante exhaled loudly as he ignored the doctor who had slipped into the room and begun an assessment of his patient. "Kyle and I. Brandy, will you marry me? Will you fill our lives until there's no vacancy left for anyone else, anything else?"

"I...I—"

"Aw, hell, say yes," the doctor, a large man in every way, interrupted, his stethoscope dangling from his Dumbo ears. "Because this busy little rascal's gonna need a momma *and* a daddy—to keep a close eye on him."

"You mean...?" Dante began, his eyes wide and gleaming like gold coins as he turned to the doctor.

The doctor nodded, raising the crib rail back up. "Yes, I mean. He's going to be just fine. We'll run a few more tests, another CAT scan, x-ray, some blood work, just to be certain, but take my word for it," he winked as Kyle squirmed away from him, "he's going to be driving you to do something as crazy as going and getting married, in no time."

Dante threw his dark head back and chuckled with shear relief. "Can we hold him now?"

"Not until the lady answers your question," the doctor replied, bushy brows jiggling and eyes sparkling mischievously as he sauntered from the partitioned room whistling a light tune.

Dante turned expectant eyes on her while Kyle took a sudden interest in Winnie the Pooh on his gown.

"I…I don't know what to say. I was just getting ready to ask if you wanted to buy out my half of the inn. I was…" Brandy rose and went to look out at a murky, slushy Chicago.

Dante came to stand behind her, placing his hands on her shoulders. Rubbing gently there where months of tension had gathered, he whispered in her ear, "The inn is ours together. Say yes."

Brandy closed her eyes, savoring the feel of his warm hands upon her, his hard body so near, the pleading tone to his voice. She turned slowly around to face him. "But your partnership here in Chicago. How do we—"

"What, did you think I was commuting to Chicago everyday?" he shrugged.

"I—um, hadn't thought of it," she returned a shrug of her own. "I guess I assumed you were taking another temporary leave or something." *In order to torment me*, she added silently.

"No," he chuckled softly. "I'm moving my practice to Mystic. I've dissolved my partnership ties."

Her eyes became enormous pools of green. "You would do that?"

"I already have," he pulled her to him, his arms encircling her possessively. "Brandy, I've come to realize," he began, his hands tracing patterns over her back, "that Kyle *and* you are the most important things in my life."

His hands came up and around to hold her jaw. Singeing her with a warm gold stare, he nearly moaned, "I love you."

It took her a moment to absorb his words, but only a moment, for her arms slid around him and she was suddenly clinging to him as if he would vanish if she didn't. "Did I hear you right?" she breathed, her face buried in his shirt.

"Yes, darling. I love you. I think I've loved you since I first saw your picture years ago in Ian's office."

She was stunned, in complete shock. Gripping his tie, she tilted her head back and asked with a raspy tone, "You're not just saying that, just doing this because it's what Julie wanted?"

He laughed softly, his eyes squinting with warmth. "Julie was a manipulative woman, that's for sure. I'll admit that she was right, but I'd never do or say something that I didn't mean in my heart."

"Oh, Dante!" Brandy wailed, raising on tip-toe to plant an intense kiss on his lips. "I love you too! I don't know why, I don't know how, so soon after Ian…but I just know that I do. I—I have so much room left in my heart, for you, for Kyle…I don't know how it happened!"

"But it did. So," he pulled her tight against him. "Will you, or won't you, marry me?"

"Yes, Mommy, yes!" Kyle clapped his hands, a bubbly giggle erupting from him.

They both turned to see him standing in the crib, his hands gripping the bars, and the IV tubing stretched taut across the crib in his effort to be near his parents.

"Yes," Brandy replied with a snicker. "I'll marry you, Dante. But first," she escaped his embrace and went to lower the crib rail, "I need desperately to hold him in my arms."

Epilogue

Brandy stood before her husband-to-be on the rear balcony of the inn. It was a glorious spring day with a cerulean, clear sky, a warm breeze carrying the scent of dogwood and firs, blooming mums, and freshly cut grass. Her wedding day had begun at the birth of a radiant pink and orange dawn, when she'd been clearing Ian's files, his mail, his documents, simply him, from her life. Finding the credit life insurance policy, a policy that would pay off the mortgage to her beloved bed and breakfast, she'd fallen to the office floor in a hysterical fit of laughter. All those worries over paying her debts, keeping her dream alive...*poof!* Gone forever. Ian had given her the perfect parting gift.

And it was a perfect day for a wedding.

Maxine, Natalie, Boomer, Rachelle, and all of her staff stood in attendance, as a local preacher officiated before them. Dante, dressed immaculately in a black suit and tie, simply took her breath away. This dashingly handsome man would be her husband in minutes, and she still had to wonder if she were in a dream. Kyle stood between them in a tiny suit to match Dante's, impatiently wiggling, watching in awe as a blue jay soared overhead, teaching its young to fly, to hunt for seed, to play. How could life get any better? she wondered as the minister began the ceremony.

"The Lord, our God, works in mysterious ways, as evidenced by these two before us..."

Dante turned to see the love pouring from her eyes, eyes that matched the green of the surrounding Wisconsin countryside that he'd grown to cherish. She was beautiful, breathtaking, and she was *his*. Adorned in a simple ivory dress, it was one that emphasized every curve, every valley. But there would be time for that later, after he'd presented her with that special wedding gift that he'd been working on since December, a gift that would arrive any minute now.

Looking across the rolling green fields and pastures beyond their inn, his eye caught the old oak tree that stood proud and tall near Julie's grave. He'd looked out for her all those years, but in the end, she'd known what was right for *him*. He missed her terribly, wished fervently that she were here to share in the joy of this day, in the fruits of her devious labor, but he was comforted that she lay resting near his new home.

A breeze whirled around him, gentle, fresh, invigorating. *I love you, big brother. Congratulations!* he heard her voice echo across the Wisconsin valley. And this time, he was certain it was her, knew he wasn't imagining it, and he smiled warmly, silently returning the endearment.

"Dante, you may kiss your bride," the reverend said with finality.

"You can just bet that I will," Dante replied ardently, drawing her against him. "I love you," he whispered for her ears only, his lips devouring hers in a much too passionate kiss.

But Brandy didn't care if he took her right here and now. She returned the kiss with equal enthusiasm, tossing her bouquet aside.

Natalie looked down in surprise at the bunch of fresh flowers that had landed perfectly in her hands. "Oh Lord…"

Boomer, standing proudly beside her, whispered in her ear, "Fate is merciless, isn't it?"

"You two stop that right now," Maxine warned, planting a sharp elbow in Natalie's side. The last thing she wanted was Natalie, the level-headed one of her two daughters, to go and do something as crazy as Brandy was doing right now. Why, it was shocking, she a widow for just over a year. But then, Brandy had always been impulsive and irresponsible, Maxine thought sourly.

"Excuse me…" came a voice at the back of the intimate gathering of friends and family.

Brandy and Dante broke reluctantly from one another, and all eyes turned to the strange young man standing at the rear of the balcony. He was tall and slim of build, with strawberry blonde, shortly cropped hair. Even from where she stood, Brandy could see the aqua blue of his eyes, crisp and clear as the sky above them, blue just like…

"Brandy," Dante reached for her hand, planting a butterfly kiss on her knuckles as he snared her with a warm look. "This is my wedding gift to you."

"This?" she glanced around in confusion. "This what?"

He raised a hand to the young man, motioning him over. "Brandy, meet Joshua Templeton. He's been discreetly residing over at the cottage for the past week or so."

The lad stepped forward as Dante faded into the background. "Congratulations on your wedding," he studied her, remembering the green of her eyes, recalling how they could sparkle like glimmers of rain on the grass.

Brandy searched Dante out in the small crowd. He stood there behind Joshua, hands clasped before him, silent, offering no explanation. "Well, thank you, Mr. Templeton," she began, looking boldly back at him. "But forgive me. I—I'm not sure I know you."

He smiled softly, his young handsome face lighting with a twinkle in his lucid eyes. "You know me," he assured her, reaching for her hands. "You know me as…Brian."

Brandy swallowed an enormous, painful lump. Vaguely, she heard Maxine and Natalie gasp. "Brian? Y-you said Brian? You m-mean, you're…?"

"I'm your brother," he said simply, pulling her near and kissing her on the cheek.

"*Brian!*" Maxine screeched, barreling forward, shoving Brandy aside. "You're Brian, my Brian?"

"Yes, ma'am," he looked closely at the woman, knowing instantly who she was, for Dante Saxon, his new brother-in-law, had filled him in on the family dynamics.

Natalie glided forward, placing a trembling hand on his cheek. "You're truly our brother?"

He knew who she was as well. "Yes, Natalie. I'm your brother," he affirmed her words, accepting a heartfelt hug from his big sister.

Brandy stood behind them in shock. "I hired a private investigator," Dante explained, approaching her from behind and wrapping his arms around her.

Everyone closely studied Dante, realizing that he was offering an explanation for this unbelievable turn of events.

"Your husband, Maxine," he turned glowing eyes on his new mother-in-law, "it seems, played a role in Brian's disappearance."

Maxine gasped, her hand coming to her chest. "You're lying!" she accused.

"No," Brian offered further information. "He's not lying. When Dante's man located me, my parents confessed to paying your husband a huge sum of money if he would turn me over to them. You see, they were wealthy, but unable to have children. Your husband—my biological father—met them as part of a crew that was remodeling the Templeton home. After overhearing them in a heated argument about being unable to bear a child, your husband offered to sell me to them. They accepted the proposition."

"No…" Maxine cried as Natalie enfolded her mother in her arms. "He wouldn't…"

"Yes, ma'am—er, Mother, he did."

At the one word she'd longed to hear for nearly sixteen years, Maxine untangled herself from Natalie's comforting embrace. As for her husband's terrible deed, she would address that later. But for now, she turned to Joshua and asked with red-rimmed eyes, "You're truly my Brian?"

When he nodded and opened his arms to her, she flew into them, clinging to her son, studying his handsome face and showering him with kisses. "I'm so sorry for what he did, so sorry…" she whispered.

"It's okay," he held her as if he'd always known her. "I've lived a very privileged life. I'm just sorry I never knew what they'd done."

When the wedding guests fell silent, and everyone stood wiping tears of joy, Maxine reluctantly released her son. Seeking out her youngest daughter, she stepped forward, eyes downcast. Dante released Brandy, prodding her forward toward Maxine.

Brandy dreaded the words that were about to come. Hopefully, it would be the last emphasis of her irresponsibility. Hopefully, it would be the final dig.

"Brandy?" Maxine's pained eyes rose to meet hers. "Honey, I'm sorry," she croaked, tears flowing anew. "I've put you through hell all these years. I blamed you, only a child yourself when this happened. And all the time, it was your father who'd been the one responsible."

Brandy went white with shock. She glanced over her shoulder at Dante's pleased expression. "I…I don't know what to say," she replied hesitantly to Maxine.

"Say you'll forgive me," Maxine choked. "Say we can start over."

All it took was for Brandy to see the genuine remorse…and love…in her mother's eyes. Raising her arms to encourage an embrace, she accepted her mother into her life. "You're forgiven, Mother," she cried softly, sighing as, for the first time since she was a child, she felt her mother's arms around her.

Through blurred tears, she laid her cheek on her mother's shoulder and sought out her husband, standing there all handsome and proud and truly happy for her. He winked at her, promising a future full of love and surprises.

"I love you," she silently mouthed to him across the small crowd as her life came together full circle.

And she did. With all her heart and soul.

No vacancy? There had been a day in her life, not so long ago, that she had thought there was no room left in her heart for anything else but her own grief and despair. But now she rejoiced in the fact that she had endless room in her heart, a bottomless spring of love for her handsome new husband, a mischievous two-year-old little tyke, a loving mother and sister, a brother risen from the dead, and the child that was growing within her womb.

Miracles happened in Mystic. She wasn't infertile as she'd always thought, and in the future, she would fill the inn with many of Dante's children.

But there would always be room for more.

Ian MacKay's spirit hovered over the ceremonial gathering. "Do you suppose she still loves me?" he asked, turning to seek out Julie's energy at his side.

"Everyone loves you, Ian," she chuckled, feeling a heavenly sense of contentment as she watched her brother pluck Kyle up and pull Brandy into a loving pose for the photographer. "But she does have it pretty bad for Dante."

The misty form of Ian's handsome face frowned as he heard Brandy whisper something to her new groom. "She just told him she's pregnant with his child."

"I know," Julie sighed, truly looking forward to the upcoming journey to heaven. It had been a long several months in purgatory, and both she and Ian had just received their calling to return home. "It's going to be a girl, a sister for our Kyle. A striking beauty with her father's dark coloring and her mother's gorgeous green eyes."

There was a long, contented silence.

"Julie?" Ian asked as they began to fade into the ethereal dimension.

"Yes, Ian, love."

"Do you suppose there's going to be room in heaven for us?"

As the inn faded, shattered into a million star-like pieces before them, they went toward a neon-green light that wrapped them in a sweet warmth.

Julie smiled softly, encapsulating her spirit around the only man she'd ever loved. "If there's no vacancy in heaven, Ian," she suffused her spirit into his, kissing him with her life-core, "then we'll just go back to the inn and be one big happy family together."

"No," Ian accepted her into him, then reciprocated his warmth to her. "I don't think I want to go back."

"Why ever not?" Julie spread her soul throughout the universe and let the light pull her in, even as she sailed on the wave of rapture that Ian was giving her.

"Because my eternity is now with you." His energy exhaled heavily as he continued to absorb her into him like a warm sponge. "I'm sorry for so much in my past life," he added so very gently, she wasn't certain she'd heard him correctly.

Julie looked ahead as they floated into a room of nothingness, yet glowing with love and light. "Well, Ian," she moved toward the essence of understanding and compassionate judgment. "I think you better save all your repentance for Her."

"Her?" he glanced about, sailing through the plane behind Julie's spirit.

"Yes, our maker," Julie's voice was soft, echoing with bliss as she was urged closer to eternity. "She's beautiful!"

"She is?" Ian perked up instantly, his soul searching for that which had always nourished it: Beautiful women.

"The inn is full now, Ian," she watched her life spin about her, accepting her misgivings, glad for her good deeds. With a snap, she was forgiven and allowed entry into paradise. "If you don't want to go back, now's the time to change your ways," she called out to him through the narrow gate of thriving energy.

His soul inhaled deeply. He could feel the tempting caresses of a celestial home that far surpassed any gratifications of the physical Earth they'd just left behind. "Did I ever tell you, Julie, my love, how very sorry I am...?"

About the Author

Titania Ladley has been a reader and writer of romance novels for over two decades. She has a degree in Nursing, and has experience in the hotel/motel business, a plus in aiding in the depiction of a bed and breakfast setting in her novel, *No Vacancy*. She is passionate about her work as a writer, and is currently working on three new romances and a fictional children's chapter book.

Married for seventeen years, she lives in the St. Louis, Missouri, metropolitan area with her husband, sixteen-year-old boy/girl twins, and a ten-year-old son. Her husband's career has relocated them to many settings such as Texas, Illinois, Iowa, and Florida, a factor that has enriched her writing and given her inspiration for other works of fiction.

0-595-23793-2